**"We probably should have gone to your cabin. Mine is shabby compared to yours."**

Michael took off his coat, his gaze never wavering from hers. His look was as soft as a caress. "Your cabin doesn't interest me right now."

She swallowed. "Oh."

He unbuttoned his shirt, the heated flame in his eyes keeping her still. A sensual sizzle electrified the space between them and it was only when he removed his shirt that Noreen remembered she was still fully dressed. She reached behind her for her zipper.

Michael abruptly held up his hand. "Don't move."

Noreen blinked, surprised. "Why?"

He crossed the room and stood behind her. "Because I've wanted to undress you all night and I'm not going to let you deny me that pleasure."

Then slowly, teasingly, he pushed the straps of her top off her shoulders, and slowly unzipped her skirt and let it fall to the floor.

## Books by Dara Girard

Kimani Romance

*Sparks*
*The Glass Slipper Project*
*Taming Mariella*
*Power Play*
*A Gentleman's Offer*
*Body Chemistry*
*Round the Clock*
*Words of Seduction*
*Pages of Passion*

Kimani Arabesque

*Table for Two*
*Gaining Interest*
*Carefree*
*Illusive Flame*

---

## DARA GIRARD

fell in love with storytelling at an early age. Her romance writing career happened by chance when she discovered the power of a happy ending. She is an award-winning author whose novels are known for their sense of humor, interesting plot twists and witty dialogue.

When she's not writing she enjoys spring mornings and autumn afternoons, French pastries, dancing to the latest hits, and long drives.

Dara loves to hear from her readers. You can reach her at contactdara@daragirard.com or P.O. Box 10345, Silver Spring, MD 20914.

# *Pages* of RASSION

## DARA GIRARD

KIMANI™ ROMANCE

To my fans!

 KIMANI PRESS™

ISBN-13: 978-0-373-86185-9

PAGES OF PASSION

Copyright © 2010 by Sade Odubiyi

www.kimanipress.com

Printed in U.S.A.

Dear Reader,

Welcome to the second book in my Ladies of the Pen trilogy about three writing friends—Suzanne, Noreen and Claudia—and their rocky roads to romance. You've already met Suzanne in *Words of Seduction,* and now *Pages of Passion* tells you Noreen's story.

The quote "Oh, what a tangled web we weave when first we practise to deceive!" by Sir Walter Scott best sums up the premise of this story. It is a story about deception. When I was a kid I enjoyed the game of charades, and that game gave me the perfect idea for this novel about two people pretending to be someone they're not for different reasons.

Noreen Webster pretends to be someone else because she needs a vacation. Michael Vaughn pretends to be someone else because he needs excitement. Both characters don't think they need love, but Fate has other plans—and when these two meet, they certainly get more than they bargained for! *Pages of Passion* shows the ultimate game of charades with a dash of mystery, exotic locales and lots of hot, flaming passion. Enjoy!

Thank you for your continued support. Be sure to look for Claudia's story in my next Kimani Romance novel, *Beneath the Covers,* in April 2011.

All the best,

Dara Girard

# Chapter 1

*North Carolina*

"Absolutely not."

"Please, Noreen. It will be fun."

"I'm not switching places with you, Arlene."

"We've done it before."

"Years ago."

"I really need your help."

"No." Noreen Webster made a swift, dismissive gesture with her hand then turned back to her computer screen. She sat in her home office surrounded by a floor-to-ceiling black walnut bookshelf filled with hardcovers and paperbacks and a contemporary, clear glass desk crowded with miniature figurines, numerous stacks of papers and an assortment of Post-it notes. Framed covers of her seven published books were displayed on her wall next to numerous writing awards. "Now, go away. I have work to do." Noreen rested her hands on the keyboard ready to start typing but before she could hit a key, her sister spun her swivel chair around.

"Please, Noreen," Arlene said, her tone more urgent than before.

Noreen glared up at her sister. Except for the lack of glasses—her sister didn't wear the thick, dark-framed ones Noreen favored—and the expression—Arlene looked more determined than annoyed—she could be staring at herself in a mirror. And what she saw was a petite woman dressed to accentuate her curvaceous figure, with big, brown eyes, mocha-colored skin and a head full of light brown curls that she struggled to manage with a red headband. Of course, that's where the similarities ended, because Noreen would never be caught wearing a tight, short, red jean skirt and a bedazzled blouse that said Cutie Pie. Her sister looked like a high-school senior instead of a woman of twenty-nine. Although they were identical twins, they were on opposite sides of the spectrum.

Noreen glanced down at the dark pair of blue jeans and oversize T-shirt she wore. Even as children, the differences in their personalities were apparent. While Arlene had spent most of the day primping in front of a mirror, Noreen had been busy finding a quiet spot to read the novels she loved and disappearing into her favorite stories. Their differences became even more obvious when, after the age of six, they were no longer forced to dress the same.

Noreen looked up at her sister again and shook her head. "N. O."

"Just hear me out." Arlene held out her hands before Noreen could protest further. "Please."

Noreen sat back in her chair, placing her elbows on the armrest, and sighed, resigned. "Fine." She waved a finger. "But I'll only listen on one condition."

"What?"

"That what you're asking me to do has nothing to do with Clive."

Arlene rested a hand on her hip, the bracelets on her wrists clicking together. "His name is Clyde."

Noreen shrugged, unconcerned.

Arlene frowned. "I think you say his name wrong on purpose."

Noreen blinked. "I guess I'm just hoping he won't last long. Just like the others."

"I don't know why you don't like him. He's different from all the rest." Her sister touched her chest. "I know it in my heart."

Noreen stifled another sigh. Her sister's "heart" was never accurate. Arlene had a terrible history with men. She seemed to be attracted to men other women sensibly left buried under a rock. She'd dated brutes, perverts, ex-cons and men who promised to leave their wives and never did. Arlene was unlucky in love, but Noreen couldn't blame her. She was unlucky in love too and had survived a bitter divorce to prove it. However, Arlene told everyone she knew that her perfect man was out there, and like a child who believes in fairies she never lost hope; Noreen, on the other hand, believed in Mr. Right as much as she did in Santa Claus.

"I wish you wouldn't be so cynical. You've only met him twice. He's always been nice to you, and look at the bracelet he bought me." Arlene held out her arm and twisted several bangles dangling from her wrist.

Noreen looked and frowned. "Which one is it again?"

Arlene pointed to a silver bracelet. "This one. He said it will bring me good luck and he never wants me to take it off. Isn't it beautiful?" She didn't give her sister a chance to reply. "He's sweet and handsome and charming," Arlene said in a dreamy voice while she toyed with the bracelet.

Noreen shook her head in pity. "Most jerks are handsome and charming. You should know that by now."

"And a lot of wonderful men are too. Look at the man your friend Suzanne married."

Noreen didn't want to. The recent marriage of her best friend, Suzanne Rand (now Gordon), who was also a writer, should have put a dent in her cynicism but it hadn't shifted. While she knew her friend was happy and her husband appeared to be a perfect match for her, their love seemed to be an exception. Like a pink rose that happens to grow in a bed of weeds. She didn't want to talk about her friend's wedded bliss.

"What do you want?" Noreen asked, eager to change the subject. "I'm listening as long as what you want has nothing to with Clive—Clyde," Noreen corrected when Arlene frowned.

"It does," her sister said then rushed on before Noreen could interrupt. "But if you'll just be quiet for a second I'll explain."

Noreen adjusted her glasses and nodded. "Go ahead."

Pleased that she finally had her sister's attention, Arlene grabbed a chair nearby and sat down. "He wants me to deliver a package to an eccentric client in St. Lagans."

"And?"

"And I said I would. Everything is all set for me to travel next week, but I haven't been feeling well and don't think I can make it."

Noreen gave her sister a cursory glance. "You look fine to me."

Arlene bit her lip. "Today's a good day." She cleared her throat. "The thing is…I think I might be kinda pregnant."

Noreen jumped out of her seat. "Kinda pregnant? That's impossible. You either are or you aren't."

"Sit down and just be calm."

Noreen remained standing, resting her hands on her hips. "Are you or aren't you?" she demanded.

"I am."

Noreen sank back into her chair like a lead balloon. "I see."

"I think," Arlene added sheepishly.

Noreen's tone sharpened. "You don't know?"

"The first test said 'yes' so I tried again and the second said 'no.' The nurse told me I'm probably early in my pregnancy and getting false positives *and* negatives.

So I made an appointment with a doctor, but they can't fit me in until the end of next week. I just can't handle things right now. Clyde doesn't know and until I'm sure..."

"So just tell him you can't do it."

"What reason can I give him? If I said I'm sick, he might want to take me to see the doctor himself. He's funny that way. Sometimes I think he keeps track of my cycle more than I do. But that's not the point. If I see a doctor he'll want to know why and I just don't want to have to tell him a bunch of lies."

Noreen raised her eyebrows, surprised by her sister's reasoning. "And having me pretend to be you isn't a lie?"

"Come on, Sis. I need this. It will allow me to get checked out and have some time to think things through. Especially if I am pregnant. You'll be on the cruise—I mean *I'll* be on the cruise and he'll think I'm away and it will give me the space I need to sort things out. I really want to keep him in my life and this is my chance to really impress him."

Noreen looked at her sister's perfect figure and pretty face and knew that if Clyde was like any of Arlene's past boyfriends, he was already impressed. Noreen pinched the bridge of her nose. "Okay, aside from the fact that I've never thought it wise to have an affair with your boss..."

"It's a relationship," Arlene corrected.

"Right," Noreen said, not caring about the distinction. "Why did he select you to deliver this package?"

"Because I'm special to him and he's trying to show

it. He told me so. Three months ago he had another woman, Marnie, but she never came back and Clyde was really upset about it. He said I made him believe in people again. He's never asked me to do anything and he said he trusts me and no one else. I really want to do this for him. I don't want to disappoint him."

Noreen had never suspected her sister's recent job (she'd had four in the past three years) at an antiques dealership would cause such drama. She'd been working there for less than a year and within three months she was sleeping with the boss and now she was going on a special delivery assignment for him. It didn't make sense to her, but she knew it would be hard to talk her sister out of it.

"You know I would go if I could," Arlene continued. "But I haven't been able to focus and I don't want to mess this up. Clyde really means a lot to me. He sees me as trustworthy and smart. I've never been with a man who thinks that." Her eyes filled with tears. "Please do this for me. I'll pay you."

"I don't need money," Noreen said, determined to resist any persuasion, although she felt herself weakening.

"Please, just this once," Arlene said, wiping a tear away.

But Noreen knew from experience that was a lie. Arlene had been using that line for more than twenty years. "Noreen, just this once finish my project so I won't fail Chemistry," "Just this once substitute for me," or "Just this once, lie to Daddy about where I am," and Noreen had done it. Their mother had disappeared when they were six. Except for their grandmother, Arlene was the only other female in a family of males consisting of their three half brothers, their father and an uncle. But as she grew older Noreen wondered if she'd done her sister more harm than good by always enabling her.

"I would," Noreen said in a softer tone, "but the timing is all wrong. I'm busy. I have to work on my new book." She tapped the manuscript sitting neglected on her desk. She had to completely rework it. The thought of her career caused her further distress. Her sister's life was one minidisaster after another, but Noreen knew that her career would soon follow suit if she didn't do something fast. Unfortunately, her divorce hadn't just broken her heart, it had also deadened her creativity.

She'd lost the imagination to come up with plots that had great romance and happy endings. She'd always known she wrote fiction and what she wrote had little bearing on real life, but lately, whenever she tried to write, she felt as though she was writing lies and it was definitely affecting her productivity. She was a successful, well-paid romance novelist. Her fans loved her dashing heroes and feisty heroines and how they found perfect and lasting bliss. It had been nearly two years since her divorce and she still hadn't recovered. To her, love was a farce and all men deceivers.

Noreen knew men. Sometimes more than she wanted to. They were simple creatures who preferred playthings to complex women, and as long as their basic needs were met they didn't care who gave it to them.

Their father had taught her that. Her three half brothers had come from three different women. The women had all been grateful for the opportunity to have him in their lives. Her father, Vince Webster, was a magician when it came to women. She'd discovered his secret when she'd overheard a conversation he'd had with one of her brothers.

"Women are like toys. Treat them right, play with them on occasion and they'll make you happy."

And her brothers had proven it was sage advice. They were never without women and enjoyed their company. They never made promises and it appeared that the women didn't mind.

Sometimes Noreen wondered why she'd gotten married. Maybe because her mother hadn't. It seemed like a sort of rebellion and a perfect idea at the time. But she soon learned her ex was restless and that she could never please him. He never cheated on her with another woman (or man), thankfully, but he didn't have to. The art of adventure and taking risks was his mistress and, early in their marriage, after only eight months, he told Noreen she bored him. Their marriage probably would have ended then if Noreen hadn't felt guilty and decided to fund his adventures with the money she had made from her books. Now she had to pay the bastard alimony because he claimed he helped build her career.

She'd loved him but quickly learned that love wasn't enough. Being there for him when his mother died hadn't stopped him from missing her first book signing; cooking his favorite meals hadn't guaranteed he'd arrive home at night; listening to his hopes and fears hadn't meant he'd be there for her when her car broke down. "Call triple A," he'd told her that cold, rainy night when she'd gotten stuck on the highway in the middle of winter. That's when she knew that love was painful and made a person weak. Especially women. That's when she'd made a vow to never fall victim to it again.

Unfortunately, that revelation wasn't the right attitude for a romance novelist, and her sales numbers were beginning to slip.

Her work was still publishable and she hadn't had to make any major revisions to any of her manuscripts before, but even her writing friends, Suzanne Gordon and Claudia Madison, had begun to worry when they'd spoken with her more than two months ago.

"What's wrong with it?" she asked them. She rarely asked for their feedback on her work, but when her editor had said "something was missing," she'd wanted a second opinion. The three of them sat in a chic restaurant in the heart of downtown Durham.

"The book is good. Your work always is, but your editor is right, there's something missing," Suzanne said, looking tailored and finished in gray linen trousers and a pale green fitted blouse. She was the daughter of a prominent judge and a true daughter of the South so she chose her words carefully and always kept her features pleasant.

Noreen paused, recognizing the strange note in her friend's voice. "Missing?"

"Yes." Suzanne sighed, the sigh saying more than words ever could.

"The passion isn't there," Claudia clarified, finding no need to soften her words. She was a tall, willowy woman whose bobbed, straight black hair and flowing, loose-fitting clothes gave her a bohemian air. She was a psychiatrist who'd turned her insight about relationships into bestselling books.

Noreen laughed. "Oh, you mean you want another love scene?"

Suzanne cast a hesitant look at Claudia then said, "No, it's not that. The love scenes are fine and so are the characters and plot, but it's not your usual passion-filled story. There's no emotion. The story is just sitting there flat on the page. The hero and heroine don't really seem as though they're in love. In lust, yes, but not in love. I don't see them having a real future together."

"I see," Noreen said quietly. She couldn't dispute her friend's words. As the author she knew that she didn't really see the characters living happily ever after. The hero would go on to his next conquest and the heroine would focus on her business.

"I know your divorce was hard and I under-stand—"

"Look, I'll fix it. Don't worry," Noreen said. She didn't want to talk about her divorce or its effect on her work.

Suzanne reached across the table and covered Noreen's hand. "Love does exist, you know, and there are good men out there. Men who are loving, kind and loyal."

Noreen pulled her hand away. "Right." She took a long swallow of her grape juice, wishing it was something stronger—like hundred-proof gin.

"You don't believe me," Suzanne said.

"Of course I believe you," Noreen countered, wanting her friend to let the topic die.

Claudia toyed with the long, white-gold necklace dangling around her neck. "I don't."

Suzanne and Noreen looked at their friend, baffled.

Claudia released her necklace and shook her head. "Wait, I said that wrong. I do believe there are good men out there. I just don't believe there's the perfect one. The concept of marriage is archaic."

"But you write books about families and relationships," Suzanne said.

"Because it's popular, not because I believe it. Women would be happier if their expectations weren't as high. Having a man isn't going to change your life or make it better. Freedom is the key." She looked at Suzanne. "Now, I know you're extremely happy with Rick, but your life isn't for me."

Noreen studied her friend. "You're afraid."

Claudia bristled, offended. "No, I'm not."

"You just explained why you never commit to anyone. You're afraid of disappointment."

"And you're too miserable from your divorce to try to find happiness again with any man."

"I prefer to have a set of standards to measure someone by than go with any man I find interesting."

"Maybe," Claudia said slowly, wrapping her necklace around her finger. "But I prefer companionship to going around like I'm the only woman who's ever suffered a broken heart."

Claudia's words stung. "That's not true," Noreen said, hurt.

Suzanne raised her voice. "Ladies, could we get back to discussing the novel?"

"Sorry," Claudia said. She looked at Noreen. "Here's my advice, which you can choose to accept or ignore. Take a break. Live a little, then come back to your manuscript with new eyes and you'll see what we mean."

Noreen already knew what she meant. When she'd first started writing professionally, the process had been a thrilling and exciting experience. Now it was just a job that paid the bills. The passion had died the moment her ex had walked out on her. And she didn't know how to recapture it. She had the money to do whatever she wanted, but nothing appealed to her. Not retail therapy nor a spa retreat, and she didn't want to discuss it anymore with her friends. She'd left the restaurant that day thanking them for their honesty and promising herself she'd never let herself be that vulnerable again.

She knew she needed a change, but her sister's request was out of the question. Noreen looked at Arlene and began to shake her head.

"I love him," Arlene said. "You know something about love."

*Not anymore.* "And if he loves you, he'll understand."

"I've never felt this way about anyone. My happiness lies in your hands. Please, I'll make this up to you someday." Arlene clasped her hands together. "All you have to do is pretend to be me, deliver the package once you get to St. Lagans and enjoy yourself. Oh, and take a few pictures so that when you get back I'll have something to show to Clyde."

Noreen felt herself weakening. She glanced again at her manuscript. "I don't know…."

"Sis, you need a break and it won't take much. It's a simple job. And you get to go on a cruise," Arlene hastily added, sensing her sister's interest. "Wouldn't you like to escape on a Caribbean cruise right now?"

Noreen looked out her window as the chilly late-September wind tossed dried leaves to and fro, while people bundled up in bulky fall coats and scarves scurried past.

Her silence encouraged Arlene to push harder. "Beautiful beaches and a gorgeous stateroom. I saw the brochure and the pictures are even better online. You'll get to wear great clothes. Clyde bought me this beautiful outfit that I'll let you borrow."

Noreen chewed her bottom lip. "What's in the package?"

"Oh, you don't need to worry. It's small and will easily fit in your suitcase or purse."

"What is it?"

"An antique ring with a rare gemstone. Nothing illegal. Come on, Noreen, it's not as though you've never done this before."

Noreen inwardly cringed at her sister's mention of her past. Yes, that was true. In college she'd been a courier and briefly worked for her uncle delivering items to customers until she learned what his real business was—smuggling jewelry. Not wanting to get in trouble with the law, although her uncle had tried to assure her that she wouldn't, Noreen had gotten out quickly and her decision had caused a strain in the family, especially for those who had a more lax approach regarding right and wrong.

She suspected that her family background had been part of what had charmed her ex, who knew about her father, her shady uncle, her devious brothers and her reckless sister. But he'd been disappointed when Noreen hadn't lived up to his ideal of one of the reputed "wild Websters."

But that had been a long time ago and she wasn't naive anymore. What would it hurt to do a simple delivery job and in the process enjoy a seven-day luxury cruise? She could help her sister and get a needed vacation. "Okay, fine," Noreen said. She felt she might be making a mistake, but couldn't stop herself.

Arlene squealed with delight then hugged her. "Thank you so much." She kissed her sister on the cheek. "I love you."

"Hmm. What are you going to do if…" Noreen let her words fall away and gestured to her stomach.

"If I'm pregnant?" Arlene finished when Noreen couldn't.

Noreen nodded.

"I'll be okay. Don't worry about it. You worry too much. Dad always thought so."

Noreen folded her arms, unable to deny her sister's accuracy.

"You haven't seen him lately," Arlene said, unable to let the topic drop.

"I send him cards."

"But you don't visit."

"When he sees you, he sees me."

"That's not the same."

But it was close. Most people were disappointed with Noreen after meeting vivacious Arlene, with her flashy smile, stylish clothes and scx appeal. Arlene was every color of the rainbow while Noreen was black-and-white. Everyone preferred color. "I'm busy and we never have anything to say to each other."

"But—"

"Do you want me to help you or not?"

"All right, forget it," Arlene said, not wanting to push her luck. "Everything has been taken care of and all reservations are in my name. The contact will meet you on the dock in St. Lagans. I'll call you and give you more information when I get home. You're going to have so much fun." She smiled. "Maybe you'll meet someone."

Noreen met her sister's engaging smile and shook her head. "Only in your dreams."

# Chapter 2

A week later, Noreen walked through the airport terminal in pink three-inch-high heels, a pair of straight-leg blue jeans, a pink rayon blouse that felt too small and a cashmere coat. She wore large, sterling-silver hoop earrings and her hair sleeked back. Her sister wanted her to wear an anklet, three bracelets and two necklaces, but Noreen argued she'd never get past security. "I think I'm making a big mistake," she said in a low voice.

"Only because you worry too much," Arlene said next to her. Her sister looked hideous wearing a pair of dark-framed glasses, a short-waisted wool jacket with two-inch-high clunky boots and her hair loose around her face in an unstylish manner.

Noreen glanced at her, annoyed by her sister's dowdy

appearance. "I'm not worrying, I'm just thinking, and besides, I don't dress like that."

"Yes, you do."

Noreen sighed, not in the mood to argue. She stopped at the airport checkpoint. It was time to say goodbye. She took a deep breath as if about to dive into icy water. "This is it."

"Yes. I really appreciate this."

"You'd better."

Arlene kissed Noreen on the cheek. "Try to have some fun."

"Right, and you take care of yourself."

"I will."

Noreen stiffened when she saw a familiar figure in the distance. "What is he doing here?"

Arlene spun around then gasped with joy. "It's Clyde! He's come to say goodbye. Isn't he sweet?"

*Sweet* wasn't the word Noreen would have used. To her Clyde looked as if he hated the world and most people in it. He moved in a smooth, calculated fashion and dressed with the same care. He had a trim mustache and slithers of silver in his dark hair that complemented his dark brown skin.

Noreen watched him, expecting him to walk past her and greet Arlene, but then she remembered she was playing Arlene and panic set in. She wanted to run. Clyde didn't give her the chance. He pulled her into his arms and kissed her—a deep intimate kiss that made her inwardly shudder. It had all the romance of making out with a relative. When he pulled away, Noreen forced a smile. She gripped her hands into fists so she wouldn't wipe her mouth. "This is a surprise," she said, struggling to keep her voice steady.

Clyde slid his hand down from her waist and cupped her butt. "I had to come and see my baby off."

"You really didn't have to," she said, her voice two octaves higher than normal.

"But that was very thoughtful," Arlene said.

Noreen shot her sister a look then said, "You remember my sister, uh…Noreen?"

"Sure, hi," he said, barely giving Arlene a glance, which wasn't unusual. He rarely noticed her. He was the kind of man who only paid attention to things he considered beautiful and engaging, and to him bookish, bespectacled Noreen Webster wasn't on that list. He focused his attention on the woman he thought was Arlene, which could have been romantic, but there was something in his steady gaze that chilled her. Fortunately, her sister sometimes wore colored contacts for fun, so Clyde wouldn't wonder why "Arlene" was wearing contacts now. Noreen stared back at him, trying to stay in character, but she found his clothes too neat, his skin too smooth and his eyes too probing. His cologne mingled with the slight scent of cigarettes, which didn't surprise her. She knew about his habit because she'd seen him light up an expensive brand with a gold lighter he kept in his pocket. Noreen studied him, still unable to understand what her sister saw in him. "You remember everything I told you?" he asked.

"Yes."

"Good." He pinched her butt then leaned close and whispered, "Why are you wearing panties?"

Noreen swallowed. "I didn't know you were coming."

"Did you think I'd let you go without a little goodbye present?"

Noreen felt her stomach turn and feared she'd be ill. She glared at her sister, who just smiled. She was going to make her sister pay for this. "I think I'll have a big present for you when I get back. Trust me, it will be worth the wait."

His eyes gleamed. "Is that a promise?"

"A guarantee."

He bent to kiss her again, but Noreen drew away and said, "I just have to talk to my sister for a minute." She took Arlene's arm and dragged her over to the side. When they were out of hearing she said, "I've changed my mind."

"You can't change your mind now—it's too late. The plane leaves in an hour."

"No, it's not too late. All we have to do is go into one of the bathrooms and switch clothes."

"And you'll go to the doctor for me to find out if I'm pregnant or not?" Arlene asked with sarcasm.

Noreen covered her eyes, feeling trapped. "What have I gotten myself into?"

"You're worrying again. Stop it."

"Didn't you just see what happened?"

"Yes." Arlene folded her arms. "But I'm not jealous if that's what you're worried about."

"Jealous?"

"Yes, about you kissing my man."

"*He* kissed *me*."

Arlene shrugged, seemingly unconcerned, and adjusted Noreen's headband. "Didn't I tell you he was different? No one else would come and see me off this way."

Noreen slapped Arlene's hand away. "Stop messing with my hair. I never do that to you."

"I just want you to look perfect. Remember, image is everything."

"Hmm."

Arlene rested her hands on Noreen's shoulders. "Thank you for doing this. Now, I don't want you to worry. In a week everything will be back to normal."

Noreen glanced at Clyde, who was picking lint off his jacket. "I'm not kissing him again."

"You have to kiss him goodbye," Arlene pleaded.

Noreen grimaced. "I'm going to make it fast." She darted over to Clyde and kissed him on the cheek. "Look after things for me. I need to go," she said and dashed into the security-clearance line before he could say anything. She waved wildly at them, the way she knew Arlene would. "'Bye, Noreen!"

Arlene's wave was more subdued and in character. "'Bye, Arlene. Have fun and remember you're going on the high seas."

"Why?"

Arlene pushed the glasses she wore up on her nose then winked. "Be careful of pirates."

*Virginia*

"Her name is Arlene Webster."

Michael Vaughn looked at the picture of a smiling

face staring at him from his laptop. "She's Harris's latest?" he asked, surprised. He shook his head then hit the speaker button on his phone. "Are you sure?"

"Yes."

"She looks barely legal."

"At twenty-nine, she just looks young. She's your target."

Michael stifled a groan. "I'm going to look like a pervert."

Darren laughed. "She might look sweet in photos, but this woman is a chameleon and can look 'grown up' real fast. We think that's why Harris selected her. No one would suspect her of anything. My source says she's going on the cruise to make a drop somewhere on St. Lagans."

"Do you think she knows about Harris?"

"Maybe. She seems to have a talent for bad boys and as a teen twice got picked up for shoplifting."

"Do you think she knows what the drop is?"

"That's your job to find out. We don't call you 'The Charmer' for nothing."

Michael rested his head back then glanced around his sparse surroundings. His one-bedroom apartment had all the basic creature comforts a bachelor would need and nothing more. He was hardly there so he didn't invest in it. He was used to traveling and was too restless to settle down. But last year he'd tried to retire from his previous occupation to attempt something more ordinary and suited to him—writing for travel magazines. It was fun but the wanderlust and need for excitement hadn't left him and he felt bored. His life was like a postcard—uncomplicated and well traveled.

But hearing from Darren again had been a surprise. Darren was in the business of purchasing antique items for private individuals who were extremely wealthy and did not want to go the traditional route of private sales and public auctions to get what they wanted. Whenever one of his clients—old or new—had an item stolen, they did not like to use law enforcement because they wanted their business handled with discretion. Darren was a longtime client and friend who used Michael's expertise to help him and other wealthy friends or acquaintances of his.

Recently, a very rare item had been stolen from Darren's own estate, and he needed Michael's help to retrieve it. Michael had started the business with his cousin, who had taught him some tricks about human nature when he was a teenager, and they had both become successful and rich, thanks to their many happy clients.

"Why am I helping you again?" Michael asked.

"Because you're the best and I'll make it worth your while." Darren was quiet for a moment then said, "I know you tried to retire."

"I didn't *try,* I did."

"Yes, but I thought a year was long enough for you. Am I right?"

Yes, but Michael wouldn't admit it.

Darren took his silence as agreement. "I want to get *my* property back and I want to see Harris go down. I know you can get him for me. I don't ask favors very often but I'm asking for this one. Do I need to remind you about Jen?"

Michael gripped the pen he was holding, trying not to think about his biggest mistake. "No more than you need to remind me that I have two hands."

"Sorry, but I'll resort to blackmail if I have to."

"You don't have to," Michael said. Years ago Darren had forgiven him for a major screwup, which could have ruined both of their reputations. He sighed. "I'm in."

"Good." Darren's voice lightened. "What are you doing for Christmas?"

"I never think that far."

"Come and visit me in North Carolina. It's been a while."

It had also been a while since Darren's wife had died and he knew the holidays were a hard time for him. Darren's wife had been a steadying presence in his life and Michael knew he missed her. Michael switched the speaker off and put the phone to his ear. "Sure."

"Bring a friend."

Michael's sympathy for his friend evaporated. "You know I'm not seeing anyone."

"Maybe that will change."

"What else do I need to know?" Michael asked, annoyed by the subject.

"I'll keep you posted, but there's really not much to say. Don't worry, this girl is a ditz. It's going to be one of the easiest jobs you've ever had. Flash your usual charm and she'll be putty in your hands and get you what I want."

Michael looked at the face on the screen, knowing this target wouldn't be much of a problem. "Like stealing candy from a baby."

# Chapter 3

*Island of Quita*

More than a week later, Michael was certain it would have been easier to tame a cobra than charm Arlene Webster. She'd coolly refused his invitations to have a drink, ignored his smiles and his attempts at flirtation and only answered him with monosyllabic replies. She'd shot down every chance he'd tried to get to know her and although he'd been on the cruise for three days, he'd gotten nowhere.

Michael took a sip of champagne and watched her from across the ballroom. The cruise had stopped on the island of Quita to host a masquerade ball at a local mansion. He didn't pay much attention to the festivities because he'd attended many before. All that mattered was the infuriating woman dressed up like a sorceress. Even her costume had surprised him. He'd expected her to dress up like a cheerleader or a naughty nurse, not a witch. A stylish purple wig covered her curly hair and a dark blue velvet gown with wide sleeves hugged her petite, curvy form. A black velvet mask with ostrich feathers covered the upper half of her face while spiked heels, red fishnet stockings and long black gloves completed the image.

Even in costume Michael could spot her determined "don't mess with me" walk anywhere. It didn't make sense. He never failed with women. Never. From the moment he'd begun to talk, he'd been able to charm the fairer sex. He enjoyed women and knew what made them tick—from the shy ones to the brazen ones—but Arlene Webster was proving to be an enigma. Everything Darren had told him about her felt wrong. He didn't sense that she was a ditz or Harris's latest baby doll. Yes, she definitely looked like one in the skimpy dresses and cute jeans she liked to wear, but that's where things seemed to end.

She didn't mingle with the other guests; there was an aloof, observant air about her. Had Harris changed his type? Maybe, but even if Harris had changed his type, why wouldn't the blasted woman even talk to him? He was not used to being ignored and he couldn't deny that it was starting to become a personal challenge as well as a professional one. He was going to get close to Arlene—and make sure she noticed him—no matter what. He'd just have to find her weakness.

So far his usual bait hadn't worked. She wasn't

interested in money (he'd casually displayed his Rolex watch), flattery (he'd complimented her on the color of her eyes), brains (having taken this cruise at least three times he'd told her fascinating details about the ship) or sex (his killer smile had always said plenty). He was good-looking, rich, intelligent and a little devilish, but that wasn't enough for her. He needed to find out why.

"Still no luck?" an amused voice said beside him.

Michael didn't have to look to see who it was. Joy Nedham, a colleague of his, was also on assignment and he knew whoever she had in mind didn't have much of a chance. She was gorgeous and lethal. "It's still early."

"You usually have them drooling by the first half hour."

"It appears that this one will require a little more strategy."

"Maybe you've lost your touch."

Michael took another sip of his drink. She was trying to goad him, but he wouldn't let her. He hadn't lost his touch and he was going to get Darren what he wanted. Michael Vaughn didn't fail. He'd get under Arlene's shield. He prided himself on being a chameleon able to assess a woman's needs and provide her with them. He was determined to find out what Arlene wanted and make sure she felt he was the only man to give it to her. "Come on, let's get something to eat," he said then made his way to the buffet table.

*He was the perfect hero.* Or villain. Noreen watched the striking, dark figure as he moved slowly about the mansion's elegant ballroom, trying to decide which.

The masquerade ball was in full swing with hundreds of masked vacationers wearing a varied assortment of costumes, but the dark stranger had decided not to wear a mask—he didn't need one. He wasn't classically handsome. His square jaw was too angular, his features more rugged than refined, but he was still beautiful to look at, with his rich ebony skin, trim goatee and captivating smile.

Noreen frowned at the memory of that smile. The first time he'd flashed it at her, her heart raced as though she'd just completed a marathon. Then she remembered he wasn't smiling at her, he was smiling at "Arlene" and Noreen knew that any man attracted to Arlene was bad news. She may be wearing Arlene's clothes and doing her job, but she wasn't picking up her men—no matter how intriguing—and this man certainly was.

Noreen had noticed that he smiled easily, but the expression seemed false, like a tactical play, and his features gave nothing away. She could not guess what he thought of the atmosphere around him—the glittering lights and the sumptuous food. She couldn't tell whether he was pleased or bored. And that was unsettling.

Noreen's gaze moved from his face to his costume. He wore a black hat tilted at an angle, a long black cloak with a dagger hanging from his belt, tall black boots and a dark purple shirt. His entire outfit seemed to imply he wanted to disappear into the night sky. He looked like a buccaneer or a pirate. Yes, that was it, a pirate. Not the stereotypical kind with a parrot on the shoulder or a black eye patch. He didn't need those. Even on the ship, dressed in casual khaki trousers and a blue short-sleeve shirt, he'd had a piratical air. But whether he stole hearts or was more mercenary, she couldn't be sure because he kept his true nature subtle.

But tonight it was evident. He projected the image of a dangerous man on the wrong side of the law. Yes, definitely a villain. And yet he was far from frightening—he was mesmerizing. No woman could keep their eyes off him. He was a man impossible to ignore. Men also noticed him more out of respect than fear, as if he were an alpha male entering a pack.

This wasn't the first time Noreen had seen him on the cruise. On her first day aboard she'd caught him looking at her with an intensity that made goose bumps form on her arms, but she'd looked away, not wanting to invite conversation. However, that hadn't stopped him and for the past few days he'd made several attempts to know her. He'd been kind enough to fill her in on the secret hideaways on the ship and he'd complimented her on her looks.

*Be careful of pirates.* Noreen remembered Arlene's parting words and smiled. She looked at the stranger again, knowing she didn't need any warning. She was going to stay far away from him. Whatever interest he initially had for her would disappear soon enough, because if he was looking for a cruise fling, he'd have to look elsewhere.

Noreen adjusted her gaze and focused on his new companion. It seemed that he'd already found her replacement—no surprise there. He appeared to be a man who worked fast.

The woman was dressed as a princess and looked

the part to perfection. She was tall, slender and elegant, her dusky skin matching his slightly darker shade. She laughed prettily at something he said. And as Noreen watched her, she envied her. Not the man or her looks, but the costume. The masquerade ball was a preregistered event Arlene had signed up for. Early that morning, the ship had stopped on the island for the ball and had provided each guest with a coupon and instructions to go to several local shops to get costumes. Unfortunately, none of the costumes Noreen had initially wanted fit. Even more annoying, the clerk kept trying to encourage her to wear a cheerleader outfit, which she refused. Yes, Arlene would have worn it but Noreen wanted to be something completely different. So instead of becoming the princess she'd wanted to be, she'd ended up wearing a witch's costume.

Noreen watched the couple stop at the buffet table then turned away. She'd given them—especially him— more attention than she wanted to. It was the writer in her, she thought, eager to explain her fascination with him. He was definitely character material. But men weren't her priority now. She was on the cruise to relax and enjoy herself.

Unfortunately, she'd discovered that was going to be harder than she'd expected. Her sister had lied, perhaps not on purpose, but that didn't matter. She hadn't gotten a grand stateroom, but instead a guest room the size of a pantry with a porthole that provided a button-eye view of the sea. The décor was ordinary but at least the flowers on her dressing table had been fresh and her attendant very friendly. Thankfully, the island they'd visited had been enjoyable and back on the ship the individuals assigned to her dining table were affable and amusing—two of the men kept trying to get her cabin number—but although she was surrounded by merriment she still felt numb.

In three days she'd make the drop and then head home. Noreen knew she probably wouldn't get a free cruise like this anytime soon so she was determined to squeeze out as much fun as she could before returning home to her failing story.

She needed inspiration. She needed to feel alive again, but the current environment wasn't helping. Noreen glanced around and suddenly the ballroom seemed too loud and too crowded. She escaped out into the hallway then walked out a side door to wander a small, secluded path that wound its way around the mansion's expansive grounds. It was a botanist's paradise, lined with a wide variety of tropical flowers, plants and trees providing a dizzying array of color and sensuous smells.

Although it was early evening, she could still see much of the splendid foliage, which included a baby woodrose vine—a lavender-flowered vine with soft, wooly leaves. And there was the Red Flash, a bush grown as an ornamental for its attractive red powder-puff appearance. But there was one smell in particular that attracted her. It reminded her of the Lady of the Night, a unique plant with small flowers that become aromatic only at night. The aroma, which emerges seconds after sundown, stays all night long then disappears exactly at sunrise.

Her father had introduced her to the plant after

bringing it home from one of his many trips to the West Indies, and she had fallen for its sweet, powerful scent. He had presented it and said, "Somehow this reminded me of you." Noreen stood awhile and inhaled the crisp Caribbean air, as a cool breeze gently lifted up the hem of her gown and threatened to blow off the black, feathered mask she was wearing. She rested against the bark of a palm tree and stared out at the ocean. The moonlight cascaded over the dark waves, creating a blanket of shimmering diamonds.

She didn't know how long she'd stood there before she saw the stranger again. He walked past her then down the side road. He was briefly illuminated by a streetlight then seemed to disappear, his dark clothing making him invisible in the night. She wondered where his companion was and was about to go back inside when she saw a car in the distance going too fast, its lights zigzagging down the small street.

It all seemed to happen in slow motion. And she stood paralyzed, helpless to stop the oncoming disaster. Then she saw it. The car hit him. The front hood lifted him up in the air, throwing him over the top of the car then onto the ground with a thud. Noreen wanted to scream but no sound escaped her. The screeching tires as the car sped away brought her out of her stupor. She started running toward him, but her stilettos sunk into the grass and she fell forward, tearing her stockings. Noreen stood, but her heel caught in the hem of her dress. She heard fabric rip and briefly thought that now she'd have to buy the rental dress, but she didn't care. She tore off her shoes and ran the rest of the way barefoot. By the time she reached him, the car was a dot in the distance, and a dim light fell overhead.

"Be careful," she said as she saw him struggle to sit up. Noreen took off her mask and fell to her knees beside him. "You're injured," she said gently.

He looked at her and winced. "What happened?"

"You were hit by a car. I didn't see the driver or get a license plate, but I *will* report it to the police."

"He probably didn't see me. It's my fault. I shouldn't have worn black at night."

"You were walking on the pavement," she said indignant. "He could have hit anyone. He could have hit me."

His voice tightened. "Are *you* all right?"

"Yes," she said, surprised by his question and oddly touched by his concern. "I was far away. I ran when I saw what happened. We have to get you some help and get you away from here."

"I think I can stand," he said, painfully rising to his feet.

"I don't think you should," she said, but he ignored her and stood and took a few stumbling steps forward. He would have fallen if she hadn't grabbed him. "Lean on me."

He did, causing her to nearly collapse under his weight. He was big and solid; there didn't seem to be an ounce of fat on him. He was pure muscle, like a sleek animal of prey. And very heavy. Noreen shifted in order to balance herself. "Damn, I'm sorry," he said.

"Please don't apologize."

He looked up at the mansion in the distance. "I'm not

sure I can make it to the mansion or the ship," he said then his legs buckled and he slowly sank to the ground, pulling Noreen down with him. She fell hard on her knee and bit her lip so she wouldn't yell out in pain. She scrambled out from under his arm and looked around, wondering if she should scream for help. But she knew no one would hear her. The loud music coming from the mansion filled the air, muting any other sounds, and there wasn't another building in sight.

Noreen helped him into a sitting position, resting his back against the wrought-iron gate that surrounded the mansion's grand property. It took an enormous amount of effort and her body ached from the fall she'd taken earlier. But for now nothing else mattered. She didn't care if he was a hero or a villain; whether the hard angles of his face made him handsome or not. He was a man who needed her help and for some odd reason, at that moment, it made him precious to her.

A sheen of sweat glistened on his face and she saw a gash on his forehead, where a small stream of blood slid down his face. Noreen quickly took off her torn stockings and used them to wipe the blood away. Then she noticed that his breathing was uneven. He was probably going into shock and that possibility frightened her. His eyes drooped closed. He could have a concussion. She couldn't let him fall asleep. "Do you feel sick?" She tapped his cheek when he didn't respond and his eyes slowly opened.

"What's your name?" she asked. He'd probably told her before, but she hadn't paid attention.

"Michael."

"Okay, Michael, I need you to stay awake for me, okay?"

He flashed a brief smile, although his voice was filled with pain. "You make that sound easy."

"I know, but it's important. You're going to be okay. I'm going to take care of you so don't worry. You can trust me."

Michael focused his eyes on her face, but she couldn't read the expression. "Thanks."

*Don't thank me yet,* Noreen silently thought as she searched her mind on what she should do next. "I need to call for an ambulance."

"No. I'm not that bad. I think hitting the ground hurt more than being hit by the car," Michael said, blinking quickly.

"Do you feel dizzy?"

"No." He adjusted his position slightly and winced.

"Stay still and let me get some help."

"No."

"You could have internal injuries."

"I don't think so."

"You don't know that."

"I don't care. I'd rather go back to the ship than to a hospital on this little island. If they have one, there's probably only one nurse and physician's assistant on staff, and with my luck it's likely not open."

Noreen bit her lip. She had to agree with him. She would need to get a taxi and get him back to the ship so a doctor could see him. After that she'd report the incident to the captain. She stood.

"You're leaving?"

The helplessness in his voice tore at her and she knelt back down beside him. "Only for a minute. I'm going to get a taxi. I said you could trust me, remember?"

"Yes, I guess I don't do that very easily."

Noreen took off her diamond-and-gold ring and placed it in his hand. "This ring means a lot to me, and I'd never leave it behind with anyone, but I'm leaving it with you. It's my promise that I'll be back for you, okay?"

Michael stared down at the ring then gripped it in his fist and met her eyes. "Okay."

Noreen looked down the desolate street, wishing there was someone who could stay with him, but she had no choice. She had to leave him alone. "I'll be back as soon as I can."

"I know." He lifted the hand that gripped the ring. "I have your promise."

She kissed him on the forehead as she would a scared child. It was an impulsive act and she didn't know why she did it but somehow it felt right. But the moment he looked at her, the simple action felt like so much more because he wasn't a child and his steady gaze was anything but innocent. For a second her eyes dropped to his lips, which for all his ruggedness and angles were surprisingly full and soft. She awkwardly pushed to her feet, not understanding his odd affect on her. "I'll get a taxi," she said then turned and raced down the main road. She briefly looked back and saw him make the sign of the cross. She said her own silent prayer and ran faster.

# Chapter 4

Finally, Noreen saw some lights up ahead and reached a place where a line of taxis were waiting to return the partying passengers back to the ship. She waved her arms and caught a driver's attention.

"You want a ride?" he asked.

"Yes, but I need your help. My friend was injured and I need you to help me with him." She was breathless and knew her appearance must be shocking, but she didn't care about that. She had to get help for Michael. Fast.

"I can call—"

She waved away the suggestion. "No, I just need to get him back to the ship. Now. Please follow me." She turned and ran back in the direction from which she'd come.

The driver followed in his car. When they arrived

where Michael was, they both helped him into the cab. Noreen sat in the backseat with him. He slid down, resting his head on her lap.

She stiffened, surprised.

"Please," he moaned, sensing her hesitation. "This feels good. I promise I won't go to sleep."

Noreen swallowed, staring down at his profile. He had short spiky lashes and some gray in his dark hair. He was likely closer to forty than thirty. She wondered where he'd been walking to and what had happened to his companion. After a few minutes she realized his breathing was too even. She gently pinched his cheek. "You promised you wouldn't fall asleep."

"Right," he said in a groggy voice. "I'm not."

"Where were you going?" she asked, determined to keep him awake.

"I was just walking."

"To nowhere in particular?"

"Yes."

"Do you still have my ring?"

"Yes, it's in my pocket."

"Good." Her sister would never have forgiven her if she'd lost the ring their father had given her. Noreen moved Michael's cape aside and slid her hand into his pocket, retrieving the ring. She hastily put it on.

He moaned.

"Did I hurt you?"

"No." He was quiet then said, "You've done it before."

"What?"

"Picked pockets."

He was right. Her uncle had taught her when she was a child. He'd introduced it to her like it was a game, and she was surprised how much she'd remembered. "I wasn't picking your pocket. I was getting what was mine."

"Same action, different intention. You're good."

"Good?"

"I've never had someone take something from me and enjoyed it."

"Hmm," Noreen said, unable to think of a suitable reply.

Finally, the taxi arrived at the dock and stopped in front of the ship. "Stay here. I'll get some help."

Michael sat up. "I can make it on my own."

"You're too—" Noreen stopped talking because he wasn't listening to her as he opened the cab door.

"My wallet...I need to pay the driver."

"I'll take care of it," Noreen said. "If you'll just wait—"

But of course he didn't and climbed out of the car. "I'll pay you back," he said.

He might not be a hero or villain but he was definitely stubborn. With the taxi driver, Noreen helped Michael to the ship. They had gotten halfway up the plank when two crew members saw them and came to assist. Immediately, the ship's doctor was called and the ship's captain contacted. In the chaos, Noreen managed to pay the taxi driver and offered a generous tip, provided a crew member with detailed information about the accident and Michael's injuries, and instructed the captain to contact the police without delay.

Three hours later, as Noreen paced the sick bay while Michael lay on a sterile white bed and drifted in and out of consciousness, she wondered what she was doing there. He was fine, so she should leave him. But for some reason she couldn't. She liked being around him. He fascinated her. She briefly stopped pacing and stared at him in wonder. He was enormous, like a fallen lion, majestic and beautiful. Something that usually frightened others intrigued her. She was surprised she'd been able to move him; he had felt like a cement block and while she knew she'd feel the pain of falling and helping him tomorrow, for now she didn't care.

*What are you all about, Michael? Why are you so taken with Arlene? Is it the clothes?* Noreen bit her lip and studied him. Perhaps she'd misjudged him. Maybe he wasn't the player or bastard she'd first pegged him to be. Had Arlene's luck changed? Could this be her chance to get her sister away from that no-good Clyde? She leaned closer to the bed. He had a nice profile. And he was kind. Even though he'd been in pain he'd offered to pay for the taxi.

What if he'd tried to talk to "Arlene" because he'd been lonely? Maybe he'd just lost his wife and decided to come on the cruise for a second chance, Noreen thought, trying to come up with a history for him. Maybe he was trying to date again and was working on his technique. He probably ran a large company selling office supplies…no, hardware. Yes, that suited him. He'd taken the business over from his father and doubled its profits within months. He had no children, but definitely wanted them in the future. If Arlene was pregnant she'd need a man who would be a good father and if she wasn't pregnant, making babies with him would be a lot of fun.

Noreen started to pace again. *Where had that thought come from?* He did not suit her. Any interest she had in him would only be for Arlene's sake. She should just go. But for some reason she didn't want him to wake up alone. She felt responsible for him, even though he was evidently arrogant and stubborn. Tonight she'd acted completely out of character for Arlene. Arlene would have run screaming in the other direction and not gotten herself involved. Her sister hated the sight of blood and was usually always the one being rescued, *not* rescuing others.

Not that Noreen would consider herself involved. Just concerned. He was like a story that she had to finish. Noreen assured herself that once she knew he was all right, the story would end.

"Do you have a problem keeping still?" he muttered, his voice sounding like a bass drum.

Noreen stopped. "Oh good, you're awake." She walked over to his bed and stared down at a pair of hazel eyes surrounded by soot-dark lashes. "Do you know where you are?" She didn't give him a chance to answer. "You're in the sick bay and it's a little over…" She checked her watch. "Eleven-thirty at night. You were in an accident, but I spoke to the doctor and she assured me that you are going to recover. Your ribs are bruised but not broken. You didn't suffer a concussion or any major head trauma. They gave you a sedative to help you sleep and pain medication." She saw a slight smile curve his lips. "What?"

"Nothing, please continue."

"I spoke to the captain and they will address this issue. They have decided that the next time the company hosts a party at the mansion they will close off the street. I'm still very upset. You could have been killed, and that idiot hit you and just drove off. Thank goodness the car was designed with a low front, so you were scooped up rather than hit full-on, and fortunately you're in great physical condition. That's an observation, not a compliment." She was babbling, but she couldn't seem to stop; his unnerving stare made it impossible. "Also I'm glad that your dagger was plastic. What if you'd fallen on it and stabbed yourself? But I guess since it was covered with a sheath that likely wouldn't have happened." She took a breath and smoothed out a wrinkle in his bedsheet. "My name is No—Arlene Webster and I only came here to make sure you are all right. And you look great, uh, a little worse for wear," she quickly amended. "But that's to be expected, right?" She took a step back. "And I'm not saying anything you don't already know so I'll just—"

"You really were worried about me," he said as though he couldn't believe it.

"Of course. It was an awful thing to see." Her eyes suddenly felt moist as she thought about the possibility that he could have been killed.

"Thanks for everything."

"Anyone would have done the same." When he winced, she asked, "What are you doing?"

"I want to sit up," Michael said, struggling to do just that.

"Here, let me help you." Noreen adjusted the pillows then helped him sit up. He was bare from the waist up and beautifully made. She couldn't keep her eyes from falling to his muscled physique. He'd felt like stone, but the touch of his skin felt smooth beneath her fingers. "You're hot," she said, touching the side of his neck. "I wonder if you're running a fever."

Michael raised an eyebrow and his beautiful eyes twinkled with a dangerous gleam. "If I'm hot, it's not because I'm running a fever."

Noreen felt heat on her cheeks but kept her voice neutral. With him she felt anything but numb and that was unnerving. "Do you need anything to drink?" She gestured to the table beside him. "I had them put this water and an ice bucket here for you and it's within reach so you can get to it at any time. The most important thing in healing is being comfortable." She arranged the pillows behind him then gently pushed him back and grabbed the sheets and tucked them in around him. She was about to straighten a pillow behind his head again when she felt him staring at her. She met his gaze and her skin tingled. "What?"

"You're just not what I expected."

"What did you expect?"

"I don't know," he said slowly.

"Just pretend that I'm a nurse."

He flashed a quick grin. "Right now I'm pretending a lot of things."

Noreen didn't know how to reply, so she cleared her throat.

He reached out and touched her sleeve. "I like your dress. It feels so good."

Noreen looked down at her witch's costume. She'd forgotten to change. No wonder the doctor and other crew members had looked at her with amusement. But she wasn't going to blush like she knew Noreen would. She had to remember she was Arlene. Noreen rested a hand on her hip. "Only 'feels' good? Doesn't it look good too?"

Michael's eyes measured the length of her. "I was going to get to that." He suddenly frowned. "What happened to your shoes?"

Noreen followed his gaze. "Oh, drats! I forgot about them. I wonder if it's too late to go back and get them. I had to take them off when I ran after you. I fell flat on my face, the first time, like a stupid heroine in a dumb horror film. I tore my dress and cut my leg. Then when I tried to help you get up I bruised my knee and—"

His gaze sharpened with alarm. "I hurt you?"

"No," Noreen said quickly, wishing she hadn't mentioned the incident because it seemed to upset him. "It was nothing, really. I was just talking."

"Let me see it," he demanded.

"No."

"Yes."

"No, you just want an excuse to see my legs," she teased but his expression didn't change, the hard, determined gleam didn't leave his eyes. He was definitely stubborn, but so was she. "Don't worry, I'm okay," she said then quickly smiled to soften her refusal. "What are a few cuts and bruises to getting hit by a car? I'm just happy you're all right."

Michael briefly closed his eyes and mumbled *"Dios mío."*

"Are you in pain?"

He opened his eyes and grinned. "No, I'm thanking God for an angel."

"Hardly." Noreen took a step back. He looked exhausted and needed to sleep. "Well, I'll just…" She let her words trail off when he crooked his finger, gesturing her to come closer. She leaned toward him. He crooked his finger more. She bent closer and turned her ear to him in case he wanted to whisper something. Instead he placed his lips against her cheek. Just as she'd imagined, his lips were his best feature and the soft, warm touch of them on her skin made her entire body grow hot. She snapped back, her hand on her cheek. "What was that for?"

"Thank you."

"You thanked me before," she said, trying desperately to look into his eyes and not lower.

His eyes danced with humor. "I'm thanking you again."

Be Arlene, Noreen scolded herself. Arlene wouldn't be flustered by a little kiss. "I prefer cash or jewelry."

"Gold or silver?"

"I like anything that shines or sparkles."

"I'll remember that," he said, his tone serious.

Noreen cleared her throat. Time for "Arlene" to leave. "You really should sleep," she said and left before his intense gaze could convince her to stay.

## Chapter 5

His head felt as if it had been hit with a cement block and his body as if it had been flattened by a bulldozer, but Michael still had a smile on his face. He remembered staring up at the night sky once Arlene had left him alone and making the sign of the cross, thanking God for his good fortune. He'd finally figured out how to get under her hard shell. She was a nurturer and he was going to use that weakness to his advantage.

Michael couldn't believe his luck. He never suspected that of her, not from the profile he'd gotten. But he was creating a profile of his own. She had a tough exterior that hid an inner tenderness. It was obvious that she'd been hurt before and that's why she kept people at a distance, but she'd held him close in the taxicab. He sighed with pleasure at the memory. He thought about the sensual feel of velvet against his skin when he'd rested his head on her lap while riding back to the ship, her warm fingers as they flitted across his chest as she helped him while he was in bed and her soft body as she leaned over him to adjust his pillows. He would have preferred resting his head on her chest. He'd had to resist reaching up to touch her.

No, she wasn't what he'd expected. His smile quickly vanished. That was the problem. All the information he'd received about Arlene Webster didn't fit—she was petite and strong but also a bit of an airhead. That had to be an act. Arlene was no ditz. She was smart and very sweet and, surprisingly, a little shy. Michael could sense her awareness of him and her hesitation. Harris's women usually didn't hesitate and they were easy to read. He liked his women simple so he could easily manipulate them.

From what he'd observed, Arlene wasn't easy to manipulate. Something else was going on. Harris must have changed his "type" to throw them off.

Michael sighed. He thought this was going to be a dull assignment, as they usually were. He charmed a specific target and got all the information he wanted, but this was different. Somehow he knew it wouldn't be easy. It certainly wouldn't be dull. He was going to have to keep a closer eye on Arlene and he knew that he was going to enjoy every minute of it. He'd never had anyone look after him. He was used to being on his own. He hadn't expected to wake up and find her there.

And she hadn't been sitting quietly by his bedside. She had been pacing his room with untapped energy.

At that moment he could imagine putting that energy to good use. Michael felt his body respond to the thought and shook his head. No, that wasn't why he was here. No matter how tempting she was—and she certainly was tempting—he was on a job. But he planned to enjoy keeping her company.

Of course, he knew he couldn't enjoy it too much. She belonged to another man and he had enough troubles already.

She shouldn't call him. Noreen stared at the phone the next morning trying to come up with all the reasons to leave Michael Vaughn alone. She had gotten his full name when she'd registered him. He was probably fine. She had to stop worrying. Arlene wouldn't worry. He was just bruised—he would heal. He was healthy and didn't need her to harass him. No, she didn't need to call him. Of course, she could stop by the sick bay on her way to the banquet hall just to make sure he was okay. Perhaps he needed help with his breakfast or something else.

Noreen shook her head. No, she shouldn't think that way. He was probably doing very well without her. If he needed help he could call someone. There were nurses. She took a deep breath. She was supposed to be Arlene and Arlene would go to breakfast and not think about him again, at least not until he was better. Arlene liked her men handsome and strong. Not stretched out on a bed, aching with pain. The thought of him in any type of discomfort started her worrying again, but she brushed it aside.

Noreen changed into a soft violet-colored blouse and a tight rayon skirt that she had been able to lengthen a bit by taking out the hem. She looked nothing like she did last night. The dramatic makeup she had worn had been replaced with Arlene's flashy red lipstick and purple eyeshadow. She was no longer a sorceress and he no longer a pirate. Just as the night had come to an end, so had any connection between them. She had to forget him.

But she couldn't. She thought about him all through breakfast, ignoring the chatter of other guests at her table. She thought about him as she tried to concentrate on the stained-glass activity she'd signed up for and now regretted. Of all the activities listed, Noreen had hoped this one would have been enjoyable. Unfortunately, she was the only person there older than nine and younger than seventy-five. And the instructor, in order to accommodate the chatty kids (there were six of them) and the twenty or so seniors, some who had difficulty hearing, used an unnaturally high, loud, patronizing tone to explain every step.

"Now, don't forget to put enough color on your brush. And wash *all* the color out of your brush, before you use another color—or oopsy-daisy, you'll be sorry..."

Noreen was already sorry, but fortunately she was pleased with her finished product. By the afternoon she was ready for lunch, but she knew she would continue to think about Michael until she did something about it. She found a wall phone nearby and called down to the sick bay and learned that he'd checked himself out early that morning and had returned to his cabin.

After speaking to the nurse, Noreen hung up the phone and stared at it. At least that meant he was okay. But she still wanted to know if he was healing. She wanted to see him. She didn't analyze why. She got the number for his cabin and dialed.

"Hello?" a deep, groggy voice answered.

He sounded exhausted. Hadn't he slept last night and why hadn't he stayed in the sick bay a couple more days? Noreen gripped the phone. She wasn't going to worry. She probably shouldn't have woken him.

"Hello?" he asked again.

She shouldn't have called. She didn't even know what to say to him. "I'm sorry," she said, full of apology. "I think I have the wrong number."

"Is that you, Angel?"

"It—it's Arlene," she said, a little disappointed that he'd been expecting someone else.

"Yes, I know," he said in a low voice that made her pulse quicken.

"I wanted to make sure you were all right."

"I'm just waking up. I took some pain medication and it knocked me out and now I'm starving. Do you think you could get some food delivered to my cabin? My brain's still foggy."

"Sure," Noreen said, thrilled that he wanted her help. "I'll take care of everything."

She heard a smile in his voice. "I thought you would. Thanks," he said then hung up.

Noreen replaced the receiver also feeling renewed. She could help him. Fortunately, she was used to taking charge of situations and she'd take care of this one.

She called room service and arranged for lunch to be served in his cabin. Forty-five minutes later she knocked on his door with a steward following close behind. Michael called for them to enter. When she walked into his room Noreen tripped over his shoes, which he'd carelessly tossed. She picked them up and put them over to the side then tried not to stare. His stateroom was a grand suite. It made her small cabin look like a manhole. It was spacious with several large windows providing not only an exquisite ocean view, but allowing ample natural light to flood the cabin. The walls were lined with a satin-weave fabric wall covering in a soothing moon-gray. Elegant crafted wood furniture provided the perfect touch, along with natural stone-and-glass tile accents. Off to the side was a balcony overlooking the mezzanine, where guests could look at what was happening below. Noreen walked over to the window and caught a glimpse of the event that day, which featured water acrobats performing high-diving stunts.

Finally her eyes fell on him. His deep brown skin looked succulent against the dark red silk comforter and plush down pillows on his bed. He appeared just as exhausted as when she'd left him last night. He was still shirtless except now purple bruises spotted his chest and the bandage on his forehead had been redressed.

"You should have stayed in the sick bay."

"I prefer to be here. I'm feeling better, I just look bad."

Noreen decided not to argue and thanked the steward when he placed the tray on a side table and then left.

Michael looked at the crowded tray. "That looks like enough for two people."

"There is."

He smiled. "You're joining me for lunch?" Michael's smile grew wider when she nodded. "Great. It would be nice to have some company."

Noreen arranged his tray, thrilled that she'd pleased him. She then walked the short distance between them and rested the tray on his lap.

"Thanks for doing all this," he said.

"It's nothing."

"Nothing, huh? I guess my life doesn't mean that much to you," he said in a dry tone.

"No, no, that's not what I meant at all."

"Good." He winked. "I figured as much."

Noreen folded her arms. "You were teasing me."

"No, I really appreciate all that you've done. It means a lot to me. You're a special woman."

Noreen sniffed, unimpressed. She took the plastic off his juice. "I wonder if you could tell my ex-husband that."

"You were married?"

She stiffened. *Ooops.* Arlene had never been married. She crumbled the plastic in her hand. "Um…no, I mean my ex-boyfriend. We were together so long it felt like we were married."

"Is he the reason why you've not given any man on this ship a chance to get to know you?"

Noreen couldn't help a smile. "He's partly the reason."

"What's the other reason?"

"I happen to be a jerk magnet."

Michael raised his brows, offended. "Thanks a lot."

"I didn't know you then."

"And now that you know me, what do you think?"

Noreen sat at the small side table and placed a napkin on her lap. "I think you're fishing for a compliment."

"Damn right, I am. My body is bruised and so is my ego. I need some tender love and care."

"Eat your lunch."

Michael looked down at his tray and frowned. "What exactly is this?"

"Vegetable soup, French bread and applesauce. I thought you should start light."

Michael lifted the spoon out of the bowl then let the contents plop back into it. "Are you sure this is soup?"

"Of course I'm sure."

He took a sip then grimaced.

Noreen shook her head. "I'm sure it's not that bad."

"You taste it," he challenged.

"You're being childish," Noreen said, taking the spoon from him and scooping up some vegetables. "I'm sure it's fine." She took a large spoonful, swallowed and nearly choked. She cleared her throat and kept her face composed.

Michael studied her. "Well?"

She set the spoon down. "It tastes like boiled water and paste."

He bit his lip. "Please don't make me laugh."

"I'm sorry." Noreen covered her mouth, but when she met his eyes they both burst into laughter.

He winced and squeezed his eyes shut. "Stop, please."

"I'm so sorry," she said, taking the tray away. "I was just trying to be careful. You can share what I'm having. I've got enough for two." She prepared his plate, making sure to get a sample of everything—fried plantain, a fruit mixture nestled in a coconut shell, spicy jerk chicken wings and refried black beans.

"That's a relief. I thought my little angel was growing horns. Yes, that's better," he said when Noreen replaced his soup with a new plate. He took a bite and moaned with pleasure. "That's perfect."

Noreen returned to her seat. "Good."

"So you're not seeing anyone now?"

She sent him a quick look. Why was he so interested in her love life? "I'd rather not talk about myself. I'm here to get away from it all and think things through."

"So that's a yes?"

"Does it matter?"

"I like to know where I stand."

"Yes, I'm seeing someone, but it might not last."

"And you're on this cruise to get away from him and think over your relationship?"

"Something like that. Why are you so curious?"

"A man likes to know if he has any competition."

Noreen bit into her fried plantain.

"So where are you from?"

"North Carolina," she said, thankful for a safe topic.

Michael shook his head. "That explains the Southern charm, but not the accent."

"I'm originally from Boston," Noreen said, feeling a slight blush.

"That explains it. So what do you do in North Carolina?"

Noreen cleared her throat. "I'm in antiques," she said, vaguely wishing she'd paid more attention to what her sister did. "I'm really not very interesting. What about you? You don't usually see a good-looking, wealthy man all alone on a cruise ship."

"So you noticed?"

"That you're good-looking?"

Michael's mouth quirked with humor. "No, that I'm wealthy."

Noreen threw her hands up and laughed. "Okay, so you caught me. I noticed you on the first day and I was impressed."

"So impressed you'll have dinner with me tonight?" When she hesitated he said, "Please, I don't want to eat by myself."

"How about the people assigned to your table?"

He sent her a look of horror. "Have you met them?"

"They can't be worse than mine."

"I have two older women who are convinced I am the spitting image of their dead brother, Lenny."

"I have a couple of newlyweds."

He nodded. "That can be annoying, but that's not too bad."

"The newlywed husband slipped me his number."

Michael narrowed his eyes and pointed a warning

finger at her. "I swear if you make me laugh again I'll strangle you."

"Okay, then I won't tell you about Bertram."

He shook his head. "I'm scared to ask."

Noreen opened her mouth then closed it. "I'll wait until you're feeling better."

"Does that mean you'll have dinner with me?"

Noreen lifted her hand to adjust her glasses then remembered she wasn't wearing them because she was Arlene. She looked over at Michael and couldn't deny the electric thrill of attraction. She liked him.

He was everything her ex wasn't. He smiled easily and she could make him laugh and he appreciated her. He had a calm, steadying presence. They were alike in many ways except, of course, he was attracted to Arlene, like most men were. But that was okay. He was a big improvement over Clyde. And why shouldn't she have some fun pretending to be her sister?

A man like Michael would never look at Noreen. But right now she wasn't Noreen and being with him would certainly get her creative juices flowing again. He would be her Muse—from his beautiful hazel eyes to his well-made body. More than once she'd imagined crawling in bed with him. The trip was definitely starting to have its benefits.

Noreen finished her lunch then walked over to one of the large windows. She raised her arms over her head in a way she'd seen her sister do many times and got the desired response—Michael's gaze fell to her chest. "You know, the weather is great today. How would you like to sit out on the deck after lunch?" She let her arms fall.

"Get some sun." When he didn't respond, she snapped her fingers. "Michael?"

He lifted his eyes to her face. "Huh?"

She stifled a grin. "The deck? Would you like to go out on the deck after lunch?"

"Only if you say yes to dinner."

Noreen raised an eyebrow and sent him a coy smile, seeing the gleam of interest in his eyes. "Are you sure you're only asking me to dinner?"

He flashed a devastating grin. "We'll talk about dessert later."

# Chapter 6

That evening Michael wasn't smiling. He sat in his stateroom as he buttoned his newly pressed white shirt for dinner and frowned at his cell phone, remembering his conversation with Darren.

"How are things going?" Darren had asked him.

"Fine."

"You only say 'fine' when you're worried. What's wrong?"

"Nothing. It's fine. I'll give you a report later."

"If you're worried, your instincts are right."

"Why?"

"I just discovered who Arlene's uncle is." He paused for effect. "Obsidian."

Michael swore. "Obsidian" was the nickname of Langston Webster, a known smuggler who wore a pinkie ring with that gemstone and for years had eluded capture.

"She and her sister had worked for him years ago. Arlene's sister, Noreen, had gotten out first."

"Smart girl."

"Arlene wasn't. She lasted nearly a year longer before things got real hot and Obsidian went underground. What a family. Their father, Vince Webster, cons everyone he meets and sleeps his way through high society, but he's harmless. However, his brother isn't."

"So maybe she's not as dumb as we thought."

"That's what I thought," Darren agreed.

"Thanks. This helps."

"I thought so. Be careful. Remember—"

"I know," Michael interrupted with a fierce sigh. "You don't have to remind me."

"What else is going on? I can tell you're worried about something."

"No, I just had a little mishap, but I'm recovering. Talk to you later," he said then disconnected and tossed the phone on his bed and swore. Darren was right. He was worried because things weren't fine. For the first time in his career he was falling for a target. And he was falling hard.

Michael knew he was in trouble the moment he met Arlene on the deck at the pool that afternoon. He wore a pair of dark trunks and a white mesh T-shirt to cover his bruises. The lower deck was crowded. As he made his way to the pool he heard the sound of kids squealing with delight in the kiddie pool, loud splashes as people dived off the diving board and low conversations of travelers lazing on lounge chairs.

He remembered that Arlene had spotted him first and called out his name and he saw her waving at him from the pool. It had been more than an hour since they'd finished lunch and agreed to meet there. He'd needed that hour break from her to get a hold of his mixed feelings about her. He still hadn't been able to figure her out. Michael walked over to the deep end of the pool. She swam to the edge and took off her goggles then rested her arms on the side and looked up at him.

He grinned. "Couldn't wait, huh?"

"Sorry, I wanted to get in a quick swim before we met." She pointed to something in the distance. "I reserved those two deck chairs for us."

Michael turned and saw two chairs loaded with towels, books and suntan lotion. "Great," he said. He turned to her and blinked, amazed that she'd caused him such confusion before. The medication must have enhanced his attraction to her because he didn't feel that same pull now. He stared at her bright, engaging grin and big brown eyes thinking how cute she was. She wore a dark blue swim cap that made her look as harmless as a pixie. He wasn't in any danger. Yes, he was in complete control again. He inwardly laughed at himself.

Then she got out of the water.

He stopped laughing.

She wore a bright orange bikini—her nipples pressing against the elastic fabric like little pebbles begging to be touched. Water streamed down her body, pooling in her cleavage and sliding down her hips and thighs in a way his hands wanted to. He watched her mouth move, hypnotized by her full, wet lips. He knew she was speaking, but he couldn't hear a sound.

Suddenly she turned and walked toward the deck chairs, giving him an enviable view of her backside.

He stood, paralyzed, as he studied how the orange fabric of her bikini emphasized the seductive swish of her hips and the round curve of her butt. She abruptly stopped and turned to him. "Michael? Is something wrong?"

He quickly lifted his eyes and saw the worry on her face. "No, I—"

"Was the walk too much for you? This pool is far from your cabin. I should have thought about that." She came up to him and draped his arm over her shoulders then wrapped her arm around his waist, pressing her wet body against him. He groaned.

"Am I hurting you?" she asked sharply.

She was killing him, but it was sweet torture and the evidence of his desire was on full alert. If her hand slipped lower than his waist he was a lost man. "I don't think this is a good idea."

"Why not? Don't worry about anyone looking— it's none of their business." Arlene held him tighter. He knew she meant it as an act of reassurance, but it affected his equilibrium and he stumbled forward. "Careful, Michael. I don't want you to fall. Lean on me. Come on. You did it before," she said, leading him to the deck chair. Once they reached it she swept the items off the seat. "There you go."

Michael sat down and briefly closed his eyes.

"You really are in pain, aren't you?" she said, anxious. "And I've gotten you wet. Do you want me to help you take off your shirt?"

His eyes flew open. "No!"

She hesitated, surprised by his vehemence, then softened her voice. "Is it because of your bruises?"

He met her eyes with amazement. She was completely unaware of the effect she had on him. The expression in her eyes reflected only deep concern. That Arlene truly cared about his well-being stunned him. Who was this woman who could dress and walk like a sex kitten one moment and be Florence Nightingale the next? And why did she keep looking at him like that? As if he was special and dear to her? He could hardly remember the last time a woman had treated him with such tenderness. The last time was…no, he wasn't going to go back that far.

Her attention was becoming like a drug he was starting to crave. Michael covered his eyes, unable to meet her gentle gaze. "Yes," he lied. "It's the bruises."

"They don't look that bad, but I understand."

He sighed with relief that she'd believed him, then he felt the soft pressure of her fingers on his leg. He nearly leaped off the chair.

"What are you doing?" he asked, noticing that one of her bikini straps was sliding down. He stared at it wishing he could move it with mental energy—*just a little lower.*

She pulled it back up. "I'm going to help you. Just lean back."

"Don't. I'm fine. Really," he said then lifted his legs and swung them onto the chair to prove it. But he did the motion too fast and swore.

"You don't have to pretend you don't need help," she said then stood and reached across him.

He balled his hands into fists. Her beautiful brown body was like a tree and her breasts hung in front of him like two bright oranges ready to be plucked. He could imagine peeling off the outer layer and sucking the divine fruit underneath. Before he could further enjoy his fantasy, she pulled back and opened a towel.

He stared at her, wary. "What are you doing?"

"I'm going to put this over you."

Michael took it from her and draped the towel over his lap, glad that his trunks were loose. "It's all right. I don't need it."

She grabbed her own towel and wrapped it around herself, staring at him, unsure.

"I'm okay," he said, glancing away. He was going to kiss her if she kept looking at him like that.

"I don't—"

"So tell me about Bertram, the man at your table," he said, desperate to change the subject.

To his relief the look of worry left her face and Arlene smiled. She sat down on the lounge chair beside him. She told him about Bertram, a failed ventriloquist who tried to throw his voice and make his sock puppet talk then she did an imitation of him trying to feed it. And Michael burst into laughter and winced, begging her to stop.

"I'm sorry," she said, biting her lip.

Michael rubbed his side. "It's my fault for asking."

"I don't usually make people laugh. Maybe I should stop talking."

He shook his head. "No, I like it, just talk about something else." He pointed at her and said in a stern voice, "Just try not to be funny."

Her lips twitched but she obliged and told him other stories about interesting people she'd met on the ship. Then she told him about her eagerness to visit the islands and what she hoped to see on her high-seas adventure. At that point Michael realized he liked listening to her talk. He liked her slight New England accent and the pictures she painted with words. "You're a really good storyteller. Have you ever thought of writing your stories down?"

"Oh, um…no," she said awkwardly. "I leave the writing to my sister."

"You have a sister?" he asked, already knowing the answer.

"Yes, we're twins actually."

"Identical?"

"Yes."

He paused. "Ever switched places?"

"A few times when we were ten," she admitted. "But then my grandmother found out and made our lives so miserable we never did it again."

"Is your sister anything like you?"

"No, she's, um…what's the word?"

"Boring?"

"No," she said in a tight voice. "More reserved. She writes romance novels."

"While you live them? I bet she uses you as her inspiration."

She lowered her gaze. "No, she says her imagination is enough."

"If I had you in my life, I wouldn't need any imagination."

Arlene blushed and again she baffled him. How could a woman who wore a bright bikini blush at such an ordinary compliment?

"Tell me more about my competition."

"Why?" She took off her swimming cap and fluffed up her hair. She adjusted the towel wrapped around her.

"I want to know." Michael extended his hand and lifted her arm. "Did he give you this?" he asked, gesturing to the silver bracelet.

"Yes."

"Could I at least get a name? Or are you making him up?"

"He is not a figment of my imagination. His name is Clyde. Clyde Harris. He's an antiques dealer."

"Like you?"

"I work for him."

"That sounds cozy. A clever way to ensure job security."

She frowned. "We have a lot in common. He's also very generous, an excellent dresser and—" she faltered and reached for her suntan lotion.

"And?"

"And that's all you need to know."

"But I want to know more. How did you meet?"

She shook her head. "That's none of your business and forget about trying to get me to share anything more. You're a man of the world and our meeting is just a moment in time. I don't believe I am, or will be, the only woman in your life. Why should you expect to be the only man?"

It was a fair question that Michael couldn't answer. In an instant something in him changed. He didn't want to be just another man in a woman's life, the charmer, the playboy, the friend. His past relationships—both real and false—suddenly felt hollow. He craved something more. Something real and lasting. He didn't want to be with just any woman; he wanted to be with This Woman and he wanted to be Her Man. The one and only.

He didn't want another man to touch her, to wake up to her smile, to taste her lips. Especially when he hadn't had the chance to yet. The strength of his desire surprised him and he fought to keep it at bay. It had to be the medication that was fogging his brain. He was only going to take aspirin from now on.

"Besides," she continued. "I know more about him than I do about you."

Michael studied her then tilted his head to the side. "What do you want to know?"

She stared at him for a moment then asked, "What do you do?"

"I'm a travel writer."

"It must pay well."

"I also have various investments."

"How about women?"

He grinned. "Yes, I like to invest in them too."

She met his grin with one of her own. "Are you investing in one now?"

"Do you mean *right now* or generally?"

She raised an eyebrow, acknowledging his interest in her. "Generally."

"No, I don't have one right now, but I'm hoping to change that. Anything I invest in increases in value."

"I see," she said, with a knowing look in her sharp gaze that hit him at his core. For a moment he felt exposed, as if she was a savvy game hunter recognizing the predatory nature in him, but she didn't judge him. He knew then that Arlene may be a lot of things, but she was no ditz.

"So you're not going to tell me anything more about Clyde?" Michael asked, determined to stay focused on his job.

Arlene leaned back in her chair. "There's nothing you need to know."

"Why isn't he here with you?"

"I told you my reason before. We're giving each other space."

"Do you like keeping secrets?"

She turned to him. "Just some."

"I get a sense that you don't trust men in general." Michael paused. "Or is it just me in particular?"

"It's not you. I have a poor record."

"How bad?"

Arlene put on her sunglasses and pushed them up on her head like a headband. "The men in my life have been deceivers, betrayers, adulterers and a host of other things."

"And you expect me to fall into one of those categories?"

Her eyes searched his face, looking for something he couldn't fathom. "Let's say I hope not, but I wouldn't be surprised," she said and he saw a vulnerable look of hurt that touched him. But before he could say anything Arlene covered her beautiful brown eyes with the dark shade of her sunglasses, effectively shutting him out.

Later that night, alone in his cabin, Michael remembered that moment and scowled as he stared at his reflection in his bathroom mirror. He was one of the deceivers she'd tried to guard herself against and he hated himself for it, but he had no choice.

He splashed cold water on his face. He had to pull himself together. She was just a woman. He'd never let a woman affect him like this, especially a target, and he wouldn't start now. He could love them and leave them and usually did. He wasn't cruel. He didn't hurt anyone. He was a charmer, not a heartbreaker. He was a brief fling that made a woman feel good, and he was usually in and out of their lives before they could miss him and he liked it like that. He didn't need permanency. He was a free agent.

Michael wiped the water from his face with a towel, briefly pressing the towel against his face, remembering how Arlene had held him close. There was something different about her. Her soft warmth was like coming home. He'd never had a true place of safety. He angrily crumpled the towel into a ball and threw it at the mirror. No. He wasn't going to fall for that crap. He wasn't going to delude himself. A woman was a woman. That was all. He'd met prettier women, smarter women, kinder women, sexier women. Why was she having such an effect on him?

Because she was genuine. She lived her life and made no apologies for it. That truth rang in his mind like a lost echo. She hadn't fallen for him initially because she'd seen through his game. She took care of him because he was wounded, not to get something from him. And she talked to him without pretense—or a hidden agenda. She didn't tell him about her history with men to get pity. She told him because that was the truth. He'd been a liar so long that her honesty lured him in like a beacon of light in darkness. She made him want to be a better man.

A knock on the door took him out of his thoughts. Michael glanced at his watch. It was only eight. They'd agreed to meet at eight-thirty at the restaurant. He opened the door and saw Joy standing there.

"Darren told me to check on you," she said. "How much have you gotten?" She was dressed for dinner in a seductive red sheath dress. She crossed the room and sat down at his small table.

Michael tucked in his shirt. "Not much."

"You will. She'll fall for you soon enough."

"You think so?" he asked, with more hope than he'd realized.

Joy sent him a curious look. "They usually do. Why do you sound so surprised?"

Michael rubbed the back of his neck. "No reason."

"What's up, Vaughn?"

He let his hand fall. Joy only called him by that name

when she was determined to uncover something. "Arlene may be more complicated than we thought. She's done this before. It may be harder to get what we want."

"You always get what you want." Joy leaned back and crossed her legs. "I saw you and Arlene by the pool and it looks like you've finally gotten her under your spell." She paused and traced a circle on the table. "Or is it vice versa?" she asked while watching him as he maintained his distance.

"It's not like that," he said in a gruff voice. He took his dinner jacket out of the closet. "I haven't been myself. It's been a crazy trip. First I was hit by a car—"

Joy flattened her palm on the table and gaped at him. "What? When?"

"Last night."

She jumped out of her chair, rushed over to him and touched his face. "Oh my God! No wonder you disappeared from the party. Why didn't you tell me?" She measured him with dismay. "Are you sure you should be up?"

"I'm all right." For some reason her concern embarrassed him and he stepped away. Joy let her hand fall and composed herself. Years ago they'd had an affair. They had even flirted with the idea of marriage, but their relationship never got to that stage. Although they were now older and wiser and she was still gorgeous, Michael didn't want to get that close again. Joy must have sensed it because instead of returning to the table, she sat on the edge of his bed, providing Michael with a fabulous view of her legs.

"I'm lucky it was a sports car and not an SUV," he

said to fill the awkward silence. "I didn't call because I couldn't talk and I was drugged up until late this afternoon. Besides, Arlene brought me lunch."

"Really?" Joy asked, intrigued.

"Yes, she was the one who found me. She took care of me and checked on me today too."

Joy lifted her brows. "I see."

"Look, I'm just playing my part. I've finally found a way to get to her and I'm going to use it."

"Right." Joy folded her arms. "Ah, now everything's becoming clear. I see your problem."

"You do?"

"Yes, she's not Harris's type."

Michael nodded, glad that she agreed. "Exactly. That's what I thought."

"She's yours."

Michael froze and blinked. "I don't have a type," he said flatly.

A small smile curved her lips. "I think you do now."

Her superior grin annoyed him. Michael tossed his jacket on the other side of the bed and rested his hands on his hips. "You've got it all wrong." He tapped his chest. "I'm here to do a job and I'm going to do it. I can get any woman I want," he said, making a broad sweep with his hand to encompass all the women on the ship. "And I've gotten plenty. I don't need to take someone else's woman." He lifted his jacket and started to put it on, then took it off and threw it on the bed. "And even if I did, I wouldn't want one of the dumb, gullible women

Harris uses as his carriers." He shook his head. "No way. I'm smarter than that."

Joy gave him a look of pity.

"I am," he said fiercely. "Don't you believe me?"

"I thought you said the profile was wrong. That Arlene isn't dumb or gullible."

"That's right. She isn't. She's smart and sweet and creative. You should hear the way she tells stories. And she's not sure how she feels about Harris. I think she's trapped somehow. Maybe he has something over her and that ties her to him. But I don't think she's happy. She's been hurt and worries a lot, but I seem to be able to make her smile."

Joy's look became even more pitying.

Michael frowned. "I'm just telling you the facts. I'm not getting personal. The medication I've been on has me a little off my game, that's all. I am in control of this situation. I won't fail."

Joy stood and shrugged. "If you say so."

"I do."

"Be careful, Michael."

He smiled. "Relax, *nena*. I've got this. You know I'm always careful." And he would be. He would be objective and keep his distance. Darren wanted his property back and wanted Harris to pay. He couldn't mess that up. His reputation, his loyalty and his friendship all depended on his success. He couldn't let a woman get in the way of that. Not again. He had to be professional.

But over a half hour later as he stood outside the restaurant, he saw Arlene and knew he was in danger of losing all he held dear.

## Chapter 7

The moment Noreen saw Michael she knew she'd worn the right outfit. She didn't like Clyde, but the man had great taste. The clothes he'd bought Arlene were expensive yet subdued. The antiques business must pay very well, she'd thought when she'd opened a zippered garment bag her sister had made her promise not to open until the night of the captain's ball. Inside was a two-piece black-and-white ensemble featuring a white silk spaghetti-strap top with lace trimming and a black ruffled suede knee-length skirt—touched off with a pair of open-toed black pumps (which, luckily, were one of the more sensible pairs of shoes her sister had packed). To finish the look, Arlene had packed large eighteen-karat gold earrings shaped like leaves, a snakelike gold bracelet that could fit around Noreen's upper arm and a novelty handbag shaped like bright red lips, which would have looked cheesy on any other woman, but complemented her ensemble.

Noreen had spent nearly ten minutes staring at the outfit, debating whether she should wear it or not. Now she knew everything was perfect. His gaze slowly and seductively slid downward, taking in every aspect of her, lingering on her bare shoulders and exposed cleavage. The piratelike air had returned to him with a vengeance that no formal attire could hide. There was something inherently male and dominating in his gaze that exhilarated her.

Was it only last night that she'd stared at him from across a ballroom, wondering if he was a hero or a villain? She still couldn't be sure, but now she didn't care.

Noreen had left his cabin that afternoon feeling giddy. She went swimming just to burn up energy. He made her feel as if she could run laps around the ship, swim the ocean, dance until dawn and do two hundred cartwheels. She was falling in love with him but the thought didn't frighten her. For several days she got to be Arlene and she was going to relish being a little reckless with her emotions. For the duration of the cruise she was going to let herself believe in happy endings and finding Mr. Right.

For her, Michael was Mr. Right Now and that was enough. She couldn't have imagined a better diversion from some of the mundane activities on board. She'd cared for him, dined with him, laughed with him, been quiet with him and felt closer to him than any man she'd ever known. What amazed her was how his hazel eyes could easily twinkle with merriment, but just as quickly sharpen with an intellect that continued to surprise her. He smiled easily because he enjoyed life, not because he was shallow.

Noreen admired his easygoing ways and with him she felt free to toss her cares aside and not worry. She wondered how long she'd be able to hold his attention. She'd never held a man's interest like this. Being Arlene definitely had its perks. Their relationship—or whatever they could call it—was a dream, except when he mentioned Clyde, but she knew he couldn't help being curious. It didn't matter, because in a few days it would all be over and she was going to enjoy the now.

Only minutes before, Noreen had come down the elevator wondering if Michael would show up for dinner. Nervous, she'd come up with several excuses for him. Perhaps they'd stayed on the deck too long or he'd grown tired of her fussing over him. He'd been brusque when she'd offered to help him back to his cabin. Maybe he'd taken pain medication and fallen asleep. She sensed an attraction, but wasn't exactly sure what it meant.

At times he looked at her like an indulgent uncle and she half expected him to pat her on the head like an adult would a child. But then there were the moments when his eyes burned and she felt as if he were melting her clothes away. The second she saw him waiting outside the restaurant, Noreen knew it was going to be one of those latter moments and her heart pounded from relief and anticipation. She was a little late because

Arlene would be. She smoothed her hair to appear more composed than she felt.

"You look like a man who wants to skip dinner and go straight to dessert," she said then stared at him, surprised by her own boldness.

"Are you a mind reader?"

"Sometimes."

"Then I'd better guard my thoughts."

"Don't." She grinned, looping her arm through his. "I like them."

They walked inside and waited to be seated. "Then you know I think you look sensational," he said.

"I like to hear you say it. The outfit was a gift."

"From a male friend."

Noreen looked up at him. "Why do you say that?"

"Because no female would give her friend that outfit."

"Why not?"

"She couldn't stand the competition," he said then followed the maître d' to a table.

The dinner that evening consisted of grilled turkey with a glazed honey-mustard sauce served over rice pilaf; on the side were a generous helping of seasoned green beans with pineapple bits and freshly baked wheat rolls. While they ate, they watched several couples dancing on the dance floor.

Michael caught her glance. "Sorry, I can't dance. I don't think I'm up to it yet."

"That's okay," Noreen said with a dismissive wave of her hand. "I'm just glad you're here."

Once dinner was over, Noreen excused herself and

went to the restroom. She touched up her lipstick then stared at her reflection in the mirror. Arlene stared back. She wore an extravagant headband, dangling earrings and glittering eye shadow. "Okay, what do I do now?" The evening was still young and she'd never discussed what would happen next. Did she let him walk her to her cabin or did she go to his? *You worry too much,* she could hear her sister say. *Just play it by ear.*

Noreen nodded. That's what she would do. She took a deep breath and began making her way back to their table. She weaved around the dance floor and was close to where Michael was sitting when a man grabbed her arm and pulled her into a dancer's embrace.

Noreen stared at him, more outraged than frightened. He didn't smell of alcohol, so he couldn't be drunk, but there had to be a reason for his strange behavior. He was middle-aged with small, gray eyes and a receding hairline that didn't take away from his looks. She tried to pull away. "Let go of me."

He strengthened his hold. "Give me a minute. I have a message."

Noreen stopped struggling. "A message?"

"Yes. Watch yourself."

He had to be drunk or high. She sniffed him but he only smelled of cheap aftershave and steak. "What are you talking about?"

"You're one of Harris's girls, aren't you? You don't have to answer that. I already know the answer."

*Harris's girls?* Had she fallen into a B-level James Bond spoof? "Is he spying on me?"

"No, I'm one of Erickson's men. You're the deliverer

and I'm the insurance. I make sure the transaction goes through."

"Why would he need you as insurance? I'm just delivering a ring. Besides I know how to take care of myself and will complete the job."

"Erickson doesn't want any interruptions."

*Who was this man and why was he threatening her?*

"Well, there won't be any interruption," Noreen said, annoyed.

"I'm here to make sure of that. Keep yourself and your property safe. Thieves like ships."

"I don't know who you are, but I know what I'm doing. Trust me." Noreen didn't like the man's tone and was confused that the client had sent someone along on the cruise to keep an eye on her.

"Just remember that some people might want more from you than your pretty face."

Noreen wordlessly stared at him, no longer feeling angry, but a little frightened.

"Like I said. Watch yourself," he repeated then abruptly released her and disappeared into the crowd.

Noreen watched him go, confused. Why would there be such a fuss over an antique ring? The confrontation reminded her of some of the men she'd met years ago when she'd worked for her uncle. No, she didn't want to even consider the possibility that her sister was involved in something illegal. This probably had to do with the eccentric client, who was waiting for the ring to be delivered. She didn't have much time to reflect on it when she found out the reason for the stranger's quick departure.

"Who was that?" Michael demanded, staring past her.

It was a simple question, but his harsh tone and the cold look in his eyes revealed a ruthlessness that made her inwardly shiver. "Oh," Noreen said in a bright voice. "He was just a little drunk and wanted someone to dance with."

Michael's eyes fell to her face, dark and probing. "He didn't look drunk to me."

"Tipsy then."

Michael frowned. "He acted like he knew you."

"Maybe I reminded him of someone," she said lightly. "Are you jealous?"

"Very," he said, with a silken thread of warning.

Noreen touched his arm, surprised by the tension in him. "Forget about it. Let's go sit down."

Without warning Michael drew her into a dancer's embrace. She didn't expect the jolt of awareness when their bodies met. She'd been close to him before and had felt his body against hers, but not like this. Before, their connection had been accidental or necessary, but this was deliberate.

"I thought you didn't want to dance."

"I changed my mind," he said, daring her to challenge him.

She declined and let herself be seduced by the pulsating music and the hard form pressed against her. Their bodies moved to the slow, steady rhythm, his arm around her waist, and she felt a deep, throbbing hunger.

She wanted him. He was the perfect antidote to her malaise. She felt as if she could dance all night. He made her feel feminine and free and strong and beautiful. She rested her head against his chest, wanting the moment to last forever.

"You don't love him," Michael said, with a flat note of conviction.

Noreen lifted her head, startled, and looked up at him. "What?"

"You wouldn't respond to me like this if you did."

"What are you talking about?"

"My competition."

Noreen sighed with annoyance. "Why are we back to that?"

"Does he have something over you? If he does, I might be able to help."

"I don't need your help. It's none of your business."

"You don't love him."

Noreen met Michael's gaze, remembering Arlene. "I do in my own way and I don't have to explain it to you."

"I'm not even sure you like him."

"You're wrong."

He slid his hand up her back to her exposed flesh, his palm hot against her skin. "You're responding to me as if a man hasn't touched you in months."

Noreen's body tingled at his touch, but she kept her voice steady. "That's your imagination."

His eyes clung to hers. "I imagine a lot of things, but I'm not imagining this."

# Chapter 8

She tried to pull away. "I'm leaving."

He held her still. "Because I'm right?"

"No, because I don't need another possessive man in my life. I don't need another man to tell me what I should or shouldn't feel," Noreen said, thinking of her ex who told her she was cold. "I want to be free."

Michael's hand continued to caress her back, trailing circles that made her aware of no one else but him. "I don't want to own you," he said in a husky tone. "I just want you to admit you feel what I feel too."

"I don't have to admit to anything," she said in a weak voice and turned her face away, unable to look at him.

"I know I'm not crazy, but something about all this is driving me insane," Michael mumbled more to himself than to her. He lifted her chin, his eyes meeting hers.

"Just tell me I'm not crazy, that there's something going on between us that's more than an affair."

"I can't." Her voice came out in a choked whisper.

He grinned. "Angel, you just did."

"Okay," she reluctantly admitted. "I feel it too. It's called lust."

Michael shook his head. "This is not lust."

"How do you know?"

"I've experienced it before. Lust is an all-consuming flame that can quickly be extinguished." He dropped his tone, his voice husky with emotion. "Desire, however, is a bonfire that consumes everything it touches and right now we're both burning."

Noreen turned away again.

He cupped her cheek and forced her to face him. "If you ignore it, the fire only grows."

"I can't—"

"You're hiding something you don't want me to know." He searched her face. "But you're too honest to lie to me and I appreciate that. You can keep your secrets because I've got a few secrets of my own." He sighed heavily. "But there's something I need to know. Do—"

The booming voice of the DJ interrupted him. "Okay, people, you know what time it is. It's karaoke time!"

People started to clear the dance floor.

"We'd better go," Noreen said, relieved by the reprieve.

"Yes." Michael turned and glanced at the stage. "Do you want to give it a try?"

Noreen started to laugh at the suggestion. She'd never

make a spectacle of herself in front of people. But she knew Arlene would. "Why not?"

Noreen signed up then waited while her heart raced. She could change her mind, but she'd always wanted to sing. As a child she'd use a hairbrush as a microphone and sang in her bedroom. As she grew older she pretended to be a lounge singer draped across a piano, or a diva capturing an audience of thousands. This was her chance to make that dream come true. When her name was called, she took the stage and chose an Aretha Franklin classic, "(You Make Me Feel Like) A Natural Woman."

Light from an overhead spotlight fell on her and the crowd got quiet. Noreen gripped the microphone and briefly closed her eyes as a way of getting into character. Then she let the music take over and began to sing. The melody came through her, beautiful and clear.

Noreen looked around the room and saw she had the audience entranced, which gave her more courage. She moved around the stage and then met Michael's eyes and sang directly to him. By the final chorus she had the crowd on their feet cheering. She ended on a high note then bowed to thunderous applause.

Noreen left the stage, feeling as though she was floating and that cloud led her back to Michael. "What did you think?" she asked or rather what she would have asked if his mouth hadn't covered hers first. His lips sent shock waves through her, coaxing her and demanding a response. She met him with her own demands, deepening their kiss until it was something delicious and intoxicating.

Michael pulled away. "I don't feel like being arrested for indecent exposure," he said in a breathless rush. "But I could take you right here."

"Wouldn't the cabin be better?" Noreen asked then stopped, surprised by her boldness.

He paused. "Is that an invitation?"

"Do you need one?"

"My cabin is bigger."

"My cabin is closer," Noreen countered, ready to take her sudden courage all the way.

Michael gestured to the door as though the decision was clear. "Lead the way."

Noreen grabbed his hand and weaved her way through the crowd to the elevators, but it was a busy night and a large gathering of people hampered her progress. By the time they reached the elevator, a group of people waiting nearby and several passengers joined in congratulating Noreen on her performance. Twice she and Michael missed a car because of her new fans. At last Michael was able to secure an empty one and shoved her inside, but on the next deck another group entered and the congratulatory praise continued. Finally, after what seemed like hours, with the elevator stopping on every deck, they reached their destination. Noreen fumbled with her cabin key, trying to show a nonchalance she didn't feel. It had been nearly twenty minutes since their kiss. What if he'd changed his mind? What if the mood was over? What if he hated her cabin? Would her bed fit the both of them?

"Relax," Michael said softly, taking the key from her. "There's no need to rush." He turned the door handle.

"I'm not going anywhere." He opened the door and gestured her inside.

Noreen placed her purse on her side table, slightly embarrassed by her cramped quarters. "We probably should have gone to your cabin. Mine is shabby compared to yours."

Michael took off his coat, his gaze never wavering from hers. His look was as soft as a caress. "Your cabin doesn't interest me right now."

She swallowed. "Oh."

He unbuttoned his shirt, the heated flame in his eyes keeping her still. A sensual sizzle electrified the space between them and it was only when he removed his shirt that Noreen remembered she was still fully dressed. She reached behind for her zipper.

Michael abruptly held up his hand. "Don't move."

Noreen blinked, surprised. "Why?"

He crossed the room and stood behind her. "Because I've wanted to undress you all evening and I'm not going to let you deny me that pleasure." He pushed the straps of her top off her shoulders then slowly lowered the zipper of her skirt in a sensual fashion and let it fall to the floor. He placed his lips on the back of her neck. The soft, moist pressure of his lips soon moved to her shoulders and down to her back and up again.

"You smell good," he whispered against her neck.

"Thank you," Noreen stammered, stunned she could still speak.

He unhooked her lacy pink bra and removed it, tossing it on the ground. "Look at me."

She didn't move.

Michael rested his chin on the curve of her shoulder, wrapping his arms around her waist. "Is my Angel suddenly shy?"

No, his "Angel" was bold and daring. Noreen took a deep breath and spun around but she couldn't look at him so she focused on his chest and saw that his bruises were healing. She touched a scar on his chest that still looked sore. "You need to put Vitamin E on that."

"Do they turn you off?" he asked in an odd tone.

Her eyes flew up and met his unreadable gaze. "No, never. I just…I don't want to hurt you. Are you sure you're up to this?"

A slow smile spread over his face. "I'm definitely up to this. Unzip my trousers and I'll show you proof."

Noreen laughed. "I believe you."

He carried her to the bed and laid her down, peeling off her panties. She removed his clothes before their bodies came together. He suddenly paused and swore.

"What?" she asked alarmed.

"Please tell me you have protection."

"No."

Michael swore fiercely and checked his watch. "The pharmacy is probably closed and I didn't pack any. I didn't expect to—" He shook his head in exasperation and started to get up. "I'm going to check."

"Wait," Noreen said, realizing something.

"What?"

"I think I have some."

"You just remembered?"

"I wasn't thinking clearly, but now I am. I have some

in my suitcase." Noreen pointed in the direction of her closet.

Michael leaped off the bed and dragged her suitcase out of the closet. "Where?"

"In the inside zipped compartment." She'd just remembered that Arlene always kept extras in her suitcase, carrying case and handbag. Unfortunately, Arlene treated condoms like seat belts. She liked having them there, but rarely used them, which explained her present situation. But Noreen wasn't going to think about that now. She smiled and quietly thanked her sister. Then she remembered the package she was supposed to deliver. She didn't want him to find it by accident and ask questions.

"Wait, I'll get it," she said, shoving him aside. "Go back to bed."

He stood. "Why?"

Noreen searched her mind for a reason then seized one. "I want to make sure I have your size."

"Are you used to smaller men?" he asked, amused.

Noreen didn't turn to him because she was eye level with the part of his anatomy she needed to cover. "I'm not going to answer that." She pulled out a condom.

He took it from her and studied it. "Hmm, flavored, huh?"

She tried not to blush. Trust Arlene not to have ordinary condoms. "Is that a problem?"

He tore open the packet and rolled it on. "Not at all. You can lick me like a lollipop if you want to."

Noreen rose to her feet. "Maybe later." She wrapped her arms around his neck. "Right now all I want to taste is you." She kissed him. Soon everything else was forgotten except their desire for each other and they stumbled back to bed.

"Should I turn off the lights?" Noreen asked.

"You're not leaving this bed," Michael said in a husky tone then for the next hour made her forget her suggestion. Eventually he drew away and stared at her in wonder as his hand skimmed the side of her thigh. "I wish I knew what was going on here."

"Do you need me to explain it to you?" she said, placing a light kiss on his ear. "Is this your first time?"

"Yes," he replied with feeling. "You do something to me. I've never felt this way."

Noreen felt the same way, but was too afraid to admit it. She wiggled beneath him, wanting every part of her to touch him. "You feel *real* good."

"You cast a spell on me, Angel." He planted soft, wet kisses up her thigh.

"Angels don't cast spells."

"You were a witch that night."

"And you were a pirate."

His eyes captured hers. "I still am," he said in a velvet tone.

"Really?"

"Yes, tonight I'm going to steal another man's treasure."

"No matter the risk?"

"I like risk," he said then covered her breast with his mouth and let his tongue tease her nipple. She arched into him, every touch of his tongue and stroke of his hand filling her with a growing arousal.

"I want you," she whispered.

"I want you more."

He entered her as though this moment had happened before in another lifetime. There was no awkwardness—he wasn't too fast or too slow—it was the perfect fit and the heady thrill of it stunned them both. They whispered each other's name like a vow. Noreen shut her eyes, dumbfounded that such exquisite rapture could exist. He'd changed her. She'd been like a desert and he'd become her oasis; she'd been a dried riverbed and he'd come like a rainstorm, filling the painful dry cracks of her spirit with nourishment. He made her feel alive—whole. She'd never feel numb again. He roused her passion to a level of unfathomable ecstasy and held her close until their lovemaking was over, then they lay silent.

She touched him after a few moments had passed. The silence had stretched to something eerie. He was still with his eyes closed, but she didn't sense that he was asleep. She noticed the bruises and one looked purpler than before. "Are you okay?" she asked with a note of anxiety.

He pressed her hand against his chest. "Angel, you just sent me to heaven."

# Chapter 9

Noreen woke up the next morning, convinced that last night had been a dream. She slowly turned her head, half expecting the space beside her to be empty. It wasn't. Michael's broad back faced her and she reached out to touch him to make sure he was real. She kissed his shoulder then slipped out of bed, tripping over his shoes. She grumbled about his untidiness and moved them against the wall then went into the bathroom. She put several lubricating drops in her eyes, because her contacts were dry, then stripped down and got into the shower.

As the water cascaded over her body she felt renewed and she couldn't think about anything else except the man asleep in her bed. She thought about Michael by the pool, at dinner, watching her sing, and she let herself imagine a future with him. Soon another song came to her and she began singing a current rock hit, like a giddy schoolgirl, then she switched to "Ain't No Mountain High Enough," letting her voice echo in the small space. She sang so loud that she didn't hear the door open at first until a deep baritone joined her. Suddenly Michael appeared in the shower. Her voice died away.

"Did you forget the words?"

"No. I didn't know you could sing."

He grinned. "I can do a lot of things. Come on," he said and started to sing again, his deep, rich voice beautiful to listen to. He motioned to her to join him and she did, their voices twining together in perfect harmony. Soon they blended more than just their voices and the shower lasted over an hour.

"The ship stops at St. Barnaby today," Michael said as he sat on the bed with a towel wrapped around his waist. "Do you want to go ashore?"

"Yes," Noreen replied, tightening the towel that wrapped her petite frame while she selected clothes from her closet.

"Great, we can have breakfast on the island."

"I'm going to change," she said then disappeared into the bathroom.

Once the door was shut, Michael swiftly searched the room. Last night he hadn't cared about what she had to hide, but in the clear light of day, he had to find out what was going on. When he'd seen Arlene dancing with Arnold "The Shark" Smith, a known participant in a notorious organization, he knew this delivery was more complicated than Darren had anticipated. It seemed that

Harris hadn't only changed his type of woman, but also his M.O., and if Arlene was carrying what he thought, she was in real danger.

Michael rummaged through the room with the quick, practical movements of a professional, making sure that nothing would look out of place. Arlene was very organized and that further solidified his impression of her intelligence. She was a woman who would pay attention to details, even on vacation. Michael didn't find anything suspicious. He then went to the closet and opened the suitcase she hadn't wanted him to see. Inside he spotted two postcards, each with Harris's return address and a brief note telling him how much she missed him. Michael had a strong impulse to throw them overboard, but pushed them aside instead. They weren't his concern right now.

He carefully opened the false bottom he'd located and sighed with relief when he saw it was empty. Typically Harris would have had something stashed there. So that was good. She didn't have Darren's property. He opened a zipped compartment and pulled out a small box. He lifted the lid and saw an antique ring with a large rare gemstone. Harris didn't usually deal in gemstones; that was something Obsidian did or someone he knew was even more dangerous. Unfortunately he now had proof that she was a courier. His heart sank as his suspicions were confirmed. But he couldn't let her make this delivery. He was convinced that she didn't know how dangerous it was. Or did she?

"Sorry, Angel," he muttered to himself. "But I can't let you do this." He then carefully dismantled the ring by loosening the gemstone, and removed the interior contents, a tiny vial, and put it in his jacket pocket.

"Why don't we eat on the ship?" Noreen called out to him.

"Uh, whatever you want, Angel." Michael replaced the ring and put the box back. He knew his actions were against protocol, but he didn't care. He wasn't going to see Arlene go down. Not after what she had done for him. Once this was all over he was going to get her away from Harris and this mess. She wouldn't end up like the others.

"I thought we could save money that way," she shouted.

"We don't need to save money. If you want to eat on the island, I'll pay."

"Then let's do that."

"I'll have to go to my cabin to change."

"That's fine. Just wait for me and I'll come with you."

"Okay." Michael put everything back the way it was then quickly changed into his clothes, so that by the time Noreen came out of the bathroom he looked as though he'd been waiting for her. And she'd been worth the wait. She looked stunning in a bold animal-print skirt and a lacy white rayon sleeveless top with tiny eyelet trimming. Yes, she was definitely something he wasn't giving back.

St. Barnaby was the perfect island for travelers. It had been created specifically for cruise ships and sported a wide variety of unusual palm trees and an assortment of exotic flowers and plants. Along the beach, a large number of shaded beach chairs were staggered, and vacationers departing the ship were greeted with a steel-pan orchestra that serenaded them upon their arrival. Off to the side, the ship's entertainment committee stood by to direct passengers who wanted to go on one of the many island excursions they sponsored, or provided transportation for those passengers who wanted to participate in the many water sports available.

Noreen and Michael ended up in the marketplace, where a cacophony of sounds greeted them. There were souvenir vendors everywhere, assaulting them with their wares as they tried to make their way to the traditional shops toward the center of the island.

"Please, Miss, you haffi buy dis for your lovely husband," one vendor called out to her.

*I wish,* Noreen thought, offering the woman a smile and a polite refusal.

"Com, sir," another vendor urged Michael. "Dis pretty lady can do well with dis woven bag…"

As they navigated themselves through the stalls, Noreen couldn't believe the amount of carvings she saw everywhere (they all looked the same to her), hand-painted silk tops and skirts, and handmade pottery decorated with mother-of-pearl and exotic seashells, which the island was known for. Luckily, Michael's big frame provided her ample protection from the onslaught of vendors. Once they reached the town center, they were greeted with the wonderful aroma coming from the food vendors dotted here and there.

Everything smelled so good; Noreen was tempted

to try it all. After having breakfast at the island's only indoor restaurant, the Seaside Cove, she and Michael settled for a tropical fruit drink made from fresh pineapples, mangoes, strawberries, coconut milk and ice. Afterward, the pair decided to visit one of the island's souvenir shops, which catered to tourists and sported everything from string bikinis to water flippers, along with exquisitely designed coral jewelry—providing ample opportunities to empty one's wallet.

Noreen preferred this venue. She wasn't adept at bartering with the sellers on the street. She always felt guilty and found herself spending too much and buying items she didn't need.

Noreen was thrilled to find a little market nearby with a very jovial, toothless man who tried flirting with her. She searched his shop and picked up a small bottle of Vitamin E oil.

"What's that for?" Michael asked when he found her studying the bottle.

"For you. It will help your scars." She went to the cashier.

Michael took out his wallet.

"Put it away," Noreen said.

He hesitated. "I thought you said it was for me."

"It is, but I'm buying it."

"No, you're not." He looked at the cashier. "How much?"

"Ignore him," Noreen said before the cashier could respond. She turned to Michael. "Put your money away or I'm not getting it."

He took a few bills out and handed them to the cashier.

Noreen began to walk away. "Fine, you can put it on yourself."

"Wait." Michael snatched back the bills from the startled man and shoved them back in his wallet. "Okay, you win."

She smiled with triumph and gave the grinning owner her money and a generous tip. "Thank you."

"I don't see why—"

"It's okay," she said, taking her change. She looped her arm through his. "You'll thank me tonight."

They left the market and walked to the island's only art gallery, which also offered antiques. Noreen immediately fell in love with a series of watercolors depicting charming sights on the island. She gasped when she saw a particular signature. "It's by Winslow Homer. Oh, I would love that."

Michael studied it with a frown and called the clerk over. "How much is this?"

She gave an amount that made Noreen shake her head. "Never mind," she said. She could afford it but didn't want Michael to know. However, he didn't seem prepared to walk away. He said something to the woman in French and Noreen watched the clerk wither a little and then scurry away.

"What did you say to her?" Noreen asked.

"I called her a thief."

"Why? If that's an original it's worth every penny."

"Exactly, but it's not an original. Winslow Homer never painted anything on this island. The painting is a fake as are half of the items in here. You didn't notice?"

Heat flooded her cheeks. "I'm still learning. I didn't know you were so knowledgeable about things like that."

This time Michael looked uncomfortable. "I've picked up a few tips while traveling. It's a kind of hobby."

Noreen glanced at the clerk and nudged Michael toward the door. "We'd better leave. You've made her uncomfortable."

Michael shot the woman a look of disdain. "So what?"

"Let's not make any more of a scene," Noreen whispered then led him outside while the clerk rearranged the price label in the glass jewelry display.

"I want to show you something," Michael said, once they were outside. "It's off the regular tourist route but I think you'll like it."

"So you've been to this island before?"

"I've been many places," he said, with a note of mystery.

Noreen looked at the crowded market and the safety of being with the crowd. Then she turned to him, ready for an adventure. "Let's go."

# Chapter 10

Michael rented a motorcycle and drove down a two-lane road. Soon the tourist attractions faded away into small dots while colorful whitewashed brick houses and brightly decorated food stands came into view. He parked on the side of a remote beach. Noreen heard festive Caribbean music coming from a small stall and the aromatic smell of spicy food. Palm trees and the sound of lazily lapping waves filled the air in rhythm to the music while boats bobbed up and down in the distance.

Noreen snuggled closer to him. "Yes, this is nice."

Michael pointed. "Ah, you see that? A boat's just coming in. You know what that means?"

"No."

"Fresh seafood. Come on."

Noreen held back. It looked like a private family gathering. "We can't just barge in on them."

"They won't mind. It's a local custom. You select the food and they cook it."

Michael took Noreen's hand and led her toward the group, who greeted them like old friends. Michael talked to the fisherman about his catch while Noreen stayed to the side, watching the women, who were appropriately dressed for the day's activity. Their heads were tied with colorful bandanas and their full skirts, hiked up into their waistbands, exposed their legs.

"Ever had fish cakes?" a rather robust woman asked.

"Yes. Do you want me to help you?" Noreen asked, eager to be of service. When the woman looked doubtful, Noreen surprised them by jumping in. She grabbed the pot where the saltfish had been soaking in water overnight to remove the salt that had been used to preserve it. She then put the saltfish in a pot of water to boil. A razor-thin woman with fine features handed her several peeled potatoes, which she added.

"Where are your seasonings?" Noreen asked.

"Dis gal know what she a do!" the third woman exclaimed and handed Noreen the items she would need. Noreen added a little parsley, thyme and onion to the water. While waiting for the items to cook, Noreen enjoyed sharing some of the many recipes her Panamanian grandmother had shared with her. The four women laughed together and before long Noreen didn't feel like a tourist but a fellow resident.

After about thirty minutes, the thin woman took the

pot and drained the saltfish and potatoes through a sieve. The saltfish and potatoes were put in separate bowls and Noreen volunteered to mash the potatoes while the other woman attended to the fish. Once the two mixtures were ready, the robust woman took over and combined them in one bowl, and added finely diced onions, a clove of garlic, two sprigs of chives, diced hot red pepper and two beaten eggs. The thin woman filled a cast-iron pan halfway with vegetable oil.

Using a wooden spoon, Noreen scooped up some of the mixture and rolled them into balls with her hands. She then rolled the balls in a little flour until they were covered and dropped them into the pan to deep-fry until crispy brown.

The thin woman laughed as she watched Noreen. "Mabel. Come an look at dis little one. She fast."

Michael walked up beside her, impressed. "Either you learn fast or you've done this before."

"My grandmother was from Panama and she taught me. I can't believe I remember."

He playfully pinched her bottom. "We're going to eat well today."

She bumped him with her hip. "Do that again and you won't be eating at all."

He held up his hands in mock surrender, making all the women laugh.

Later, Michael and Noreen sat on wooden benches and enjoyed a feast of fish cakes, curried mutton, steamed green bananas, cassava dumpling stew, banana fritters and deep-fried crawfish while looking over at the water and enjoying the company of the island regulars. After eating, they walked along the beach, Noreen collected some small shells, which she put in her handbag, and then they rested under a palm tree. Michael rested his head on her lap and closed his eyes. Unlike in the taxicab, she didn't feel awkward or surprised. Being with him felt like the most natural position in the world.

She stroked his forehead. "It's all so beautiful, Michael."

"Miguel," he muttered.

"What?"

He turned and looked up at her, his hazel eyes clear. "That's my real name. Miguel Armando Vargas. Just for this one passing moment I want you to call me that."

"Miguel," she whispered then bent down and pressed her lips to his. "Why did you change your name?"

"I didn't," he said quietly, a look of pain fleeting through his eyes. "But there are reasons I had to."

She tenderly cupped the side of his face. "I'm listening."

He stared up at her for a moment then lowered his lids. "I was born in Guatemala. When I was five my mother put me on a bus and said, *'Te quiero mucho,'* basically 'I love you,' and I never saw her again." He took a deep breath. "I went to live with my grandparents in New Jersey. They died when I was seven. I lived with an aunt until I was eight then an uncle until I was nine. Finally I was sent to my cousin Undy in Texas."

"Undy?"

He smiled. "Yep. That's the name he gave himself. He took one look at me and sat me down in his living room and said, 'Miguel, you're in the South now, and in the South you're one of three things—black, white or Mexican. Now, we're not Mexican, not that I've got anything against them, but I don't feel like educating nobody. You're too dark to pass for white so you're going to be a black brother because that's where I've got my connections, so your name is now Michael Vaughn.'"

"And you didn't mind?"

"Do you think I had a choice? Besides I didn't really know what he was talking about so I went along. I was just glad to have a family and some place to stay. I idolized him. He was smart, smooth and ran three businesses. He helped me get into college, but I was restless and he knew it so he got me my first job and I never left."

"As a travel writer?"

"Uh, yes."

"Did you ever go back to see your family?"

"Twice. Once to bury my mother then to bury my father. Nobody ever explained why they sent me away. For a while I was angry with them and that's why I didn't stay in touch, but I think the reason they sent me away was because they wanted something better for me. Once I got past the anger I let myself remember them without pain. My father used to smell of tobacco and rubber and my mother of ginger and nectarines. I remember her eyes were brown and her teeth shining white."

"That's a lovely memory," Noreen said softly. "The only thing I remember about my mother is the back of her head. I don't remember her ever looking at me." When Michael didn't say anything, Noreen felt safe to continue. "She didn't say anything when she left. I have no words to remember her by. One day she was there and the next day she was gone."

Michael looked up at her with sadness. "And you never found out why?"

A bitter smile touched Noreen's lips. "She was young and had better things to do." She paused. "I think her absence affected my sister more than it did me. She's always lived her life as though she were chasing something, as if she is grasping for happiness. She's desperate for attention no matter where it comes from."

"Maybe that's why she writes romance novels."

Noreen blinked. "What?"

"You know happy-ever-after and all that stuff. She wants to believe that it exists."

Noreen nodded. She'd briefly forgotten that she was Arlene. "Right. That's probably it."

"I guess that's something your sister and I have in common. She writes fiction and I live it. I think that's why you're so good for both of us. You're real. You're true. You say, 'Hey world, here I am. Take it or leave it.' I admire that."

"I don't deserve that kind of praise."

"Yes, you do."

Noreen was quiet then said, "Thank you for sharing your story with me."

Michael sat up and pulled her onto his lap, nuzzling her neck. "I want to share a lot of things with you."

"I'm open to sharing."

"I never had a teddy bear as a child. I always wanted one and now I have one."

"You do?"

"Yes, you're my teddy bear. You're small and soft." His hand slipped under her skirt. "And fuzzy," he said, caressing the triangle of hair between her thighs. He cupped her sex. "Actually, you're better than a teddy," he said then kissed her, his palm igniting a longing deep within her as he pressed and toyed with her there until she was wet with wanting. Then he slid two fingers gently inside her and whispered, "I want to see you come." He probed and teased until he hit her sweet spot. At that moment Noreen said his name and kissed him with wild urgency, and they fell into the soft sand and kissed and caressed until the sun started to cast shadows.

Noreen reluctantly drew away. "We'd better head back to the ship."

Michael lifted himself on his elbow. "We don't have to."

She blinked, unsure if he was teasing or not. "Of course we do. We can't let the ship leave without us."

He picked up a fistful of sand then let it slip through his grasp. "We could stay here." He sat up. "I know you're running away from something and I could take care of you. I could put you up in a hotel for a few days and I'd join you once I take care of some business. I want to be here with you. We can start over. We can change our names and start with a blank slate. Wouldn't you want that, Angel?"

Noreen hesitated.

"I know you want to," he urged.

"You may be used to going to a place and changing your name and history, but I'm not." She shook her head. "I couldn't."

"Why not? It's not so difficult."

"Because I have obligations. I have a family. I have people who depend on me. I couldn't just disappear right before the holidays."

He lowered his gaze. "I see."

"You don't know how wonderful your idea sounds," she said, clearly tempted.

Michael's eyes clung to hers. "All you have to do is say yes and leave the rest to me."

"I can't," she said miserably.

"Because of him?"

"Because of a lot of things." *Like the fact that my sister might be pregnant and I couldn't desert her. That I have an ex who I pay alimony to, and a writing career I need to fix or else I'll go broke.* "My life is more complicated than you think."

He nodded and drew a circle in the sand. "Have you ever broken the law?"

"What kind of question is that?"

"A simple one. Yes or no?"

"But where did it come from? Is it because I won't run off with you?"

He wiped the circle away. "I'm curious."

"Have you?"

He shook his head, refusing to answer. "I asked you first."

She bit her lip.

"I won't judge you."

Noreen took a deep breath. "When I was younger I did some things I regretted."

"Like what?"

She narrowed her eyes. "You're not going to let this drop, are you?"

"Nope."

She sighed. "Why do you need to know?"

"I just told you my real name. I want to know more about you."

"I stole things when I was younger and I worked for my uncle."

"What did he do?"

She cleared her throat. "He was in the shipping business."

Michael burst into laughter.

She frowned. "What's so funny?"

"I never heard it called that before," he said, sobering.

"Do you know my uncle?"

"Not personally, but I looked you up and saw your connection to Langston Webster."

Noreen felt like burying herself in the sand. She remembered that story. Her uncle had been indicted on a number of charges but thankfully was never convicted. Her sister had testified and hadn't felt shy talking to the reporters and there had been two photos of her standing in front of the courthouse as if she were attending a party instead of a trial.

"If you knew, why did you ask?"

"Because I don't know everything. Every story has

two sides. Of course, now I know why you're good at picking pockets."

"I wasn't picking your pocket. I was—"

"Retrieving what was yours," Michael finished then kissed her on the forehead. "I know. What did you do for your uncle?"

"Didn't the article tell you?"

He waited and Noreen poked holes in the sand, annoyed by his persistence. "I ran errands for him," she said vaguely, not wanting to expand on it. "But I decided to do something else."

"Why did you choose the antiques business?"

"Because I like them. Discovering the history of certain pieces is fascinating."

"I understand." Michael stared out at the waves a long moment then said, "When my mother put me on the bus she gave me this." He reached into his pocket and pulled out a chain. "It's Saint Christopher. It'll keep you safe during travel."

Noreen held the small medal in the palm of her hand. "It's beautiful."

"I want you to have it."

Startled, she met his eyes. "I couldn't."

"Please." He draped it around her neck. "It's for protection."

"Do you think I need it?" she asked with a small smile.

He didn't smile back. "I know we haven't known each other long, but you can trust me. If there's something going on, you can tell me. If you're in any trouble, I can help you."

Why did he look so worried? Why would she be in danger? She suddenly thought about the stranger in the ballroom and how aggressive Michael had been when he'd seen them dancing. "I haven't spoken to my uncle in years. Or are you worried about something else?"

"No," he said, but she didn't believe him.

"I'm all right." She stood. "We'd better get back to the ship." She held out her hand and he took it and in silence they returned to where they had parked the motorcycle.

"The thought of escape is romantic," Noreen said as she straddled the motorcycle. "But I've learned one thing."

"What?"

She wrapped her arms around his waist. "Problems can follow you into Paradise."

# Chapter 11

*I love him.* Noreen sat in her cabin with her knees drawn up and stared sightlessly ahead of her. *I love him,* but this time the thought terrified her. Unlike last night, she couldn't laugh at the prospect because she didn't love in the quick, reckless way Arlene did. Arlene freely gave her heart and affections, but Noreen gave forever. She knew this feeling wasn't something she could shake free and forget, although she knew she had to. He wanted Arlene. He'd made love to Arlene and told *her* his secrets. How could she have let this happen? How could she have been so careless? She'd guarded her heart for years, determined not to give it to a man like Michael.

He'd wanted to run away with Arlene and live with her, and for a moment Noreen had allowed herself to dream. To decide to stay with him there on that island would be heaven. She could write and…

But Arlene didn't write and Michael would probably want a woman who enjoyed partying with their neighbors and entertaining guests, not spending days locked up in a room with imaginary characters, or a woman who played with porcelain figurines when she needed inspiration. He wouldn't want a woman who enjoyed fantasy films or who spent most of her time in jeans and large T-shirts. Her ex had grown bored with her and she knew Michael would too. There was no way to make it last. Maybe it had already ended.

They'd barely made it back to the ship on time and didn't say much through dinner. Afterward they gave each other a reason to return to their separate cabins— Michael said he had important business to take care of; Noreen said she had a headache. But it was her heart that ached. She clasped the necklace in her fist, remembering him draping it around her, the sound of the wind upon the waves and the touch of his fingers. Why did he have to be so wonderful? Why couldn't he just have been charming, reckless and fun? That's all she'd expected. But today he'd revealed the man beneath his carefree veneer, forcing her to share part of herself when she hadn't planned to.

And he hadn't judged her. Instead he'd sympathized about her mother leaving and made her relation to her uncle feel inconsequential, as if he were a plumber instead of a smuggler. He didn't romanticize it as her ex had done and she was grateful for that. It erased some of her shame.

Too bad she was a fraud. He deserved the truth, but Noreen knew she couldn't give it to him. Switching places had always been a secret kept between her and her sister. No one ever knew and no one could ever know. If Arlene was pregnant, Noreen couldn't do anything to jeopardize her relationship with Clyde. When she returned home she would sort everything out, but not now.

She loved him. That was the only truth she could tell him and she hoped it was enough.

The sea air brushed his face as Michael stood on the deck outside his cabin and watched the island lights grow smaller. His hopes dimmed, as well.

"Uh-oh," Joy said approaching him. "I know that look. Something is wrong."

"*El Tiburon* is on board."

"The Shark? Really?"

"Yes, I saw him dancing with Arlene."

"Did he see you?" Joy asked sharply.

"He doesn't know me, but I know him."

Joy didn't question him. She knew that Michael could move easily through a crowd unnoticed if he wanted to. He could change his appearance and voice to suit any situation. "So she's in deep."

Michael rested his arms on the railing. "I gave her two opportunities to back out."

"But she won't."

"No."

"So now everything makes sense. She's not to be trusted."

Michael stared out into the distance.

"You can't save her, Michael. She's made her choice."

He glanced up at the sky.

Joy touched his sleeve. "Do you remember Jen?"

Michael briefly closed his eyes. His jaw twitched. "Yes."

Joy leaned toward him. "Then you know how dangerous this is. You believed her and vouched for her and she nearly got you put in prison."

"I know."

"Then why are you falling for it again? You know how dangerous The Shark can be and if Harris is with him…" Her voice trailed off and she shrugged as though the answer was obvious.

"Somehow I don't think we're dealing with Harris. First, she doesn't have Darren's property."

"You checked her stuff?"

Michael sent her a look as if to say "Of course."

"I just wondered because you like her."

"I can like someone and still do my job." He tapped the railing. "Something bigger is supposed to go down on the island. If I handle this right—"

"You could shut down this ring," she finished for him. "You'd help a lot of people. Not just one." She saw his jaw twitch again, knowing his dilemma. "Arlene is smart. I've seen her. I know what she's doing. I know how to stroke a man's ego so that he thinks he's special to me. So that he trusts me. You know those tactics too."

"She's more than that."

"Is that your head talking or something else?" Joy asked, sending a significant glance down at his trousers.

"It's something else."

She flashed a smug grin. "That's what I thought."

Michael sent her a look. "It's my heart."

Joy's grin slowly faded. "You're serious."

"Yes."

Her expression grew anxious. "This isn't like you. You're scaring me, Michael."

He was scaring himself. He knew he'd taken a gamble on the island by asking Arlene to run off with him. That could have cost him, but he'd been willing to take the risk for her. He enjoyed watching her cook with the women, picking up shells and laughing, but when she'd told him about her mother, the pain had been palpable in her voice; he'd wanted to do something to see that she was never hurt again. He wanted to take her away from the memories of her mother and the awful men in her past. He didn't know why. He was too smart for infatuation and too old for a crush. He didn't know what her hold on him was, but he couldn't deny that it was there.

"I know I made a mistake in the past," he said quietly. "But I was arrogant then. I've been able to read people a lot better now. And I know she's involved but not as deep as we think." He sighed. "I just need to get her to trust me."

Joy gripped his upper arm and gently massaged it. "You're tense."

"I know."

"I think you need something to ease that tension." She kissed him.

He abruptly stepped back. "What are you doing?"

She gently touched his face. "Making you relax."

He turned his face away. "Stop that."

"You need to get her out of your system."

"Not like this."

"You enjoyed it before," she reminded him with a knowing grin.

"Years ago. It's over between us. We agreed."

Her grin fell. "You mean *you* agreed."

Michael shook his head not wanting to rehash the past. "Oy, *nena,* not now."

Joy stared at him, tears glistening in her eyes. "Do you want me to pretend for another five years that I'm not in love with you?"

Michael ran a tired hand down his face. "Let's just focus on our jobs and—"

"I don't have an assignment," she cut in with a shaky voice. "I came on this trip because I knew you would be here. Darren told me you were doing something for him and I wanted to see you. He told me he'd invited you for Christmas." She paused. "He's lonely."

"I know." Darren was a family man at heart although he'd never admit how much his wife's absence ran deep. He thrived around people and Michael knew his friend was suited to be a husband and father.

"I thought you might be lonely too," Joy said.

"I'm not Darren."

"That's true, but that doesn't mean you're supposed to be alone."

Michael sighed, saddened by her misery. They had had fun in the past and he did care about her. He smiled with boyish affection. "You're too good for me."

Joy angrily wiped her tears away. "I don't care."

"You're beautiful and smart—"

"But I'm not twenty-nine anymore," she interrupted bitterly.

His expression hardened. "That's not it."

"Yes, it is. You're blinded by Arlene's youth and her perky little body and that she laughs at your jokes and—"

"No," he cruelly cut in. "I'm blinded by the fact that she ran barefoot to reach me after my accident, that she kept me company when I was in pain, that she spent her money buying Vitamin E oil to put on my scars." His eyes blazed into hers. "Don't insult me or yourself by implying I'm suffering from some midlife crisis. You know me better than that."

Joy lowered her eyes and smiled sadly. "Yes, but it's easier to believe."

Michael cooled his temper and kissed her on the forehead. "I know," he said, resting his arm on her shoulders like a big brother.

Joy was quiet then asked, "What are you going to do about The Shark?"

"I'll come up with a plan."

"You don't have much time. St. Lagans is our next island stop."

Noreen stood motionless, trying to keep her heart from breaking as she watched Michael on the deck with the woman from the party. The Princess (as she'd nicknamed her) was striking in a full-length, bare-back, off-the-shoulder satin dress. Her shoulder-length, light brown hair with blond highlights was pulled up into an elegant chignon, and tiny white pearl earrings sparkled from her ears. She was stunning and she touched Michael in a familiar way that surprised Noreen. There was an intimacy there. Then she kissed him. He quickly moved away and the woman looked clearly upset.

Noreen watched the scene, trying to understand what it meant. Did they know each other? Had he led her on? The Princess clearly had feelings for him.

It had to be an innocent misunderstanding. He wouldn't tell her to run away with him and then be with another woman, right? But why was he with her instead of in his cabin? Was she the "business" he had to take care of? Had she already bored him? Perhaps her refusal had ruined his sense of play. Arlene would have said yes. But that's all they had been doing. Playing. It wasn't anything of substance.

"I told you to watch out."

Noreen spun around and saw the same man from the ballroom.

"It's not smart to fall for anyone on a cruise," he said. "Shipboard romances never last."

"Who *are* you?"

He held out his hand. "Mr. Smith."

She ignored his hand. "Mr. Smith? That's the best you could come up with?"

He frowned. "It's my real name."

"Is your first name John?"

"No, but you don't need to know it." He nodded toward Michael. "I bet you he's a cruise crawler and leaves a lot of broken hearts."

"I don't believe you."

"Has he already been in your cabin?" He nodded at her expression. "That's what I thought. He got what he wanted and you lost your usefulness. At least you still have the package."

"How do you know?" His blank expression infuriated her. "You searched my cabin?"

He shrugged.

"Why don't you just hand it to Erickson, if you don't trust me?"

"That's not how things work with Erickson."

She knew what he meant. Her uncle had worked the same way; he liked to have at least three people between him and what he wanted. But it didn't make sense for such behavior for a simple antique ring.

"How you spend your time is none of my business. I only report to Erickson. And I trust you because you're smart, but I don't trust him," he said, glancing at Michael again. "There's something about that guy that makes me edgy. You don't have to agree, but we both know one thing." He raised a knowing eyebrow. "You're going to bed alone tonight." He motioned to the couple and Michael had his arm around the lady's shoulders. Mr. Smith looked at Noreen then walked past her.

Noreen didn't move, but she glanced away, no longer able to look at the pair while Mr. Smith's words echoed in her ears. Who was he really? Why did he keep bothering her? Erickson's behavior was eerily similar to her uncle's, but her uncle had stopped working this kind of operation, last she heard. And why was Michael with that woman? Noreen ran to her cabin and fell on the bed in tears. Arlene had attracted another user. She squeezed her eyes closed. No, Michael wasn't a user. She didn't believe it. She'd been around her brothers and father, so she could spot one. No. What broke her heart was that as "Arlene" she'd attracted a man she could never have. Seeing Michael with The Princess only reinforced that he liked flashy, stylish women. He'd never look at Noreen. He'd treat her the same way Clyde did. She couldn't blame him for wanting The Princess. They made an attractive couple.

Today she'd felt the weight of Michael's disappointment when she'd said no to his offer. He would have had dinner alone if she hadn't suggested they eat together. She'd lost her charm. Maybe Mr. Smith was right and he toyed with women like her father and brothers did. Perhaps he had a dozen Saint Christopher medals that he gave to women. He had admitted that he knew the island. What if this is what he did all the time? Maybe he called her "Angel" because he couldn't remember her name, the same way her brothers called every woman "baby."

She was a fool. Noreen sat up and wiped her eyes. A contact popped out and she fumbled on the bed, trying to find it, keeping her "good eye" open. When she finally felt it she shook her head, glad it was disposable. Fine, she was a fool but that didn't mean she had to be one for the rest of the trip. She'd use this experience and include it in her next book. She took out her other contact and put on her glasses. Time with Michael had already provided her many ideas so at least their time together had been beneficial.

Noreen changed into something more comfortable. At home that would have consisted of sweats, but because she was Arlene she wore a light blue silk loungewear set. Her sister never dressed down. Even when they were children, Arlene hated to get dirty while Noreen loved playing outside in the grass.

Noreen sat at her side table and wrote in her journal. In her manuscript she had her heroine write a love letter. Adrienne, her heroine, was a character who had trouble expressing her emotions, and Noreen knew this would be a good way to add passion to the story. She knew it was old-fashioned, but for a character who spent most of her time distant from people, using mostly texting and email to communicate, a handwritten letter would be a more intimate and revealing activity. Something the hero could hold on to.

Noreen allowed herself to be Adrienne and imagined writing to the hero as if he were Michael and their relationship had been something more.

My dearest,
It took me three hours to decide to write you this letter, but the silence over the last few days has been torturous. Sometimes I hate you because I want you so much. I miss you. You are the first thought that enters my mind in the morning and the last thought before I go to sleep. You haunt my dreams and I know there is no cure for how I feel

about you. I want to be with you always. I love
you. I need you and I want you in my life.
Love, A

After she'd finished, Noreen took off her glasses and
rested her head back. She imagined the letter in print,
and pictured a possible cover. Perhaps it could have
a fountain pen and parchment paper with a red rose.
Maybe she could incorporate more letters throughout the
manuscript and include another love affair. Or she could
also have Adrienne send him perfume-scented note
cards that she'd slide under his door or slip in his mail
or tape to his car's windshield. Yes, that was it. Feeling
rejuvenated, Noreen decided to call room service and
ordered a pot of coffee then started on another love
letter.

A knock on the door interrupted her. Noreen scowled,
annoyed by the interruption then she remembered the
coffee she'd ordered. She left her glasses on the table and
opened the door. She saw a large blurry figure without
a tray.

"What happened?" the figure asked in Michael's
voice.

*Michael?* He wasn't supposed to be there. Noreen
opened her mouth then closed it. She didn't know what
to say to him so she did the first thing that came to mind.
She slammed the door shut.

## Chapter 12

"What the—Angel, open up."

Noreen leaned against the door, trying to figure out what to do next. "Just a minute," she said. She had to hide her glasses and put in her contacts.

He pounded harder. "Angel!"

"Just a second." Noreen raced over to her desk and grabbed her glasses and hid them in their case, which she usually kept in the bathroom. She quickly gathered up her papers and shoved them into her journal.

"I'm going to break down this door if you don't open it up."

He would. Noreen swore. She didn't have enough time to put in her contacts. She opened the door.

Michael stormed into the room. "What's going on?"

"Nothing," she said, squinting a little so she could focus on his face. It didn't help.

"Don't lie to me. Why did you slam the door in my face?"

Noreen inched toward the bathroom. "Will you excuse me a minute?"

"No."

"Michael," she said with exasperation.

"You told me you had a headache. You didn't tell me you were sick."

"I'm not."

He pointed at her. "Then why—" A knock on the door interrupted him. He spun around. "Who's that?"

Noreen's hopes lifted. It was just the excuse she needed. "Could you answer that for me? I'll be right out." She raced into the bathroom and closed the door before he could argue. She searched for her contacts and quickly popped them in then looked at herself in the mirror and nearly let out a scream. She looked awful. Her eyes were bloodshot from crying and her eyeliner had smudged, making her look like a raccoon.

"Are you okay in there?" Michael demanded.

"I'll be out in a minute."

"You have thirty seconds."

Noreen muttered something rude under her breath.

"I heard that," he said.

"Then get away from the door," she shot back. She quickly scrubbed her face then reapplied her eyeliner. Her eyes were still a little red, but she looked more presentable. Feeling better and happy now that she could see clearly, Noreen left the bathroom and saw Michael reading something on her desk.

"What are you doing?"

"'Love, A'?" He held up the paper. "What's this?"

She walked over to him. "None of your business."

His tone hardened. "Try again."

Noreen snatched the paper away. "It's personal."

"It's a love letter."

Noreen was about to say "So what?" when she suddenly understood that he thought *A* stood for Arlene. "It's not what you think."

He folded his arms. "Then explain it to me."

"It's complicated."

Michael muttered something she couldn't understand then slapped his forehead. "I'm an idiot. I really thought you were different. I believed in you, but you're used to playing with men. You've got us tied up in your spider-web. First Harris, then me and now this guy. I fooled myself into thinking you actually cared about me."

Noreen rested her hands on her hips. "What about you?"

"What about me?"

"I saw you on the deck, kissing another woman."

He stared at her, nonplussed. "I see."

Noreen let her arms fall. "At least you didn't deny it. I have to give you points for that."

"It was nothing more than an awkward moment." He took a deep breath. "We used to be lovers and—"

"And she wants you back."

"Something like that."

"I think it's *exactly* like that. Do you want her?"

"I wouldn't be here if I did."

"Really? I thought you had important business to take care of."

He frowned. "You followed me?"

"No, I wanted to see you. I had something to say."

"What?"

She waved the idea aside. "It doesn't matter now."

"You don't have to worry about her. It's over between us."

"Does she know that?"

"She does now. I made myself clear."

"Before or after you kissed her?"

He tapped his chest, affronted. "She kissed me."

"Did you enjoy it?"

"Is that what this is about?" he asked. "You saw me and thought I was cheating, which, by the way, is impossible because we haven't talked about being exclusive anyway."

"You're rambling."

He ran a hand over his face. "Damn. You must be rubbing off on me." He pointed at her. "Admit that you're jealous. That you wrote this letter out of spite because you don't want me to be with any other woman but you."

*No, I wrote that letter for a novel,* she wanted to say, but she couldn't tell him that. And she wasn't going to let him have the satisfaction of knowing she was jealous. "It was for you," she lied.

His eyes widened. "What?"

Noreen swallowed her sense of panic and searched her thoughts, desperate to expand on her lie. "I was just

imagining what I would do if I never saw you again."
She flashed an uneasy smile. "Some women write in
their diaries. I write love letters."

Michael's eyes narrowed suspiciously. "Why did you
think you wouldn't see me again?"

"You know why."

"Because of what you thought you saw or because of
Clyde?"

Noreen's cell phone rang and she grabbed it, once
again glad for an interruption.

Michael reached for the phone. "Don't answer it."

She moved it out of his reach. "It could be important."
Noreen looked at the ID and saw Clyde's number. She
silently swore. "Speak of the devil."

"It's him?"

She nodded, staring down at the phone.

"Break up with him now."

Noreen looked up at him, stunned. "I can't do
that."

"Why not?"

"I just can't."

He reached for the phone again. "Then I'll do it for
you."

Noreen stepped back. "And I'll never talk to you
again."

"Angel," Michael warned.

She knew there was one more ring before it went
to voice mail, but she had to talk to Clyde. Now. She
didn't want to have to get back to him. Arlene trusted
her to keep up the charade and keep Clyde interested.

She turned her back and walked away from Michael. "Hello?"

"Is that any way to greet me?" Clyde said.

"Sorry," Noreen said, searching her mind to figure out how Arlene would address him. "Hey, baby."

"That's better. Everything okay?"

She didn't look at Michael. "Everything's fine."

"I miss you."

"I miss you too."

Michael walked up to her. Noreen held up a warning finger and mouthed "Don't touch me."

He held up his hands in a show of obedience.

"Are you enjoying yourself?" Clyde asked.

"I'd have more fun if you were here with me," she said, imitating Arlene's coy tone.

Michael's hands fell to his hips.

Clyde laughed. "What are you wearing?"

"Your coffee's getting cold," Michael said.

"Who's that?" Clyde asked in a suspicious tone. "Is someone there?"

Noreen glared at Michael. "There's no one here. It's just the TV."

Michael sat on the bed.

"Sounded like someone was in the room."

Noreen turned away from him and lightened her voice. "Oh, yes…that's just the steward. He's delivered my coffee."

"You don't drink coffee."

Damn, he was right. Arlene hated coffee. She shook her head. "I mean hot chocolate," she said then yelped when Michael pulled her onto his lap.

"Arlene?" Clyde said, sounding worried.

"I'm still here." She elbowed Michael; he tightened his hold.

"Are you sure you're okay? You sound distracted."

Noreen removed Michael's hand from under her shirt. "I've had a long day."

"Are you sure that's all? You sound a little breath-less."

"Because you take my breath away, baby."

Michael growled; Noreen slapped his leg.

Clyde lowered his voice. "And you know what you do to me," he said.

Noreen closed her eyes, hoping he wouldn't tell her. Michael pressed his lips against the back of her neck then touched her skin with the tip of his tongue. She gripped the phone. "Um...baby, you're starting to break up. I'll try to call you later."

"Are you sure everything is okay?"

"Yes."

"You're ready for St. Lagans?"

"Definitely." Michael nipped her skin with his teeth and her body tingled. She had to get off the phone fast. "I...barely...hear..." she said, leaving out words so he'd think the connection was bad. "Better...go. 'Bye." She disconnected then turned to Michael. "You're impossible."

"Why did you tell him you were drinking hot chocolate?"

"Because he doesn't like me drinking coffee."

Michael's eyes pierced hers. "Next time you're going to tell him about me."

"No, I won't."

"Yes, you will."

Noreen wiggled off his lap and stood. "I can't. You have no idea what you're asking me."

"Yes, I do."

"There's a lot at stake. He's been good to me. I owe him. I've known him for months and you for less than a week. He's the reason I'm on this trip. He paid for everything. I can't hurt him like that. I love him. You may not understand that, but I do."

"Then why were you crying?"

"I don't know."

"Is it because you saw me with another woman?" He didn't let her answer. "Why would that bother you when you have Clyde? Don't I have the right to belong to someone the way you do?"

"You're right," Noreen said, suddenly weary. "Let's end this now. It's been fun but it's getting complicated. You can go back to your princess—"

"My princess?"

"Yes, that's what she was at the masquerade ball."

His eyes brightened. "So you noticed me then too?"

"That's not the point," she said, irritated by his amusement. "It's over. You've got whatever-her-name-is and—"

"Joy."

"What?"

"Her name is Joy."

Noreen clenched her teeth. "Does it matter?"

He shrugged. "I thought you might want to know."

"You're ruining my moment. If you haven't noticed, we're breaking up."

"Sorry, go on." He made a motion of zipping his lips.

"Right," she said, annoyed by his mocking tone. "You go back to Joy and I'll go back to Clive...uh, Clyde," she hastily corrected. "And that's it. No one gets hurt. Now if you'll excuse me, I'd like to be alone." She walked over to her side table and sat. She opened her journal and began writing.

Michael walked up to her and peered over her shoulder. "Are you writing another love letter?"

She stiffened. "Go away."

He toyed with the soft hairs on the back of her neck. "That's what you expect me to do, isn't it?"

She swatted his hand away. "There's nothing else to say."

He rested his arms on the back of her chair. "I think you have the same issues your sister has but you hide it better. You don't trust people to stay, but I promise you this." He kissed her cheek. "I'm not going anywhere."

Noreen turned to him. She desperately wanted to believe him as she sought reassurance in his eyes. But a series of questions flooded her. Were there other women in his past like Joy? How could a man who traveled a lot promise anything? Was he really all that he seemed?

But did she have a right to ask those questions when she was wearing a façade? Did the answers really matter when they probably would never see each other again? All that mattered was now. That he was here with her.

She didn't care about the reason why. And he'd proven Mr. Smith, the stranger from the ballroom, wrong.

He hadn't used her. He wanted to be with her and he'd told her the truth about the woman on the deck. She could tell him the truth too. "I'll tell you why I was crying." She took a deep, steadying breath. "I was crying because there are so many things I can't tell you. I was crying because when you asked me to stay on the island with you, I wished I could say yes. And if my life were my own, I'd follow you anywhere and that's the truth."

"I believe you," Michael said softly then he held her close. "This might be the worst mistake of my life, but I do." He kissed her on the forehead then pulled away and unbuttoned his shirt.

Noreen stared at him, curious. "What are you doing?"

"Getting ready for bed." He placed his shirt on the dresser then undid his trousers.

"Here?"

"Yes."

"But your cabin is nicer."

"I know." He pulled down the sheets. "It's bigger, better decorated and more expensive." He climbed into bed and pulled up the covers to his waist. "There's just one problem with it."

"What?"

He smiled at her. "You're not in it." He nodded to her desk. "Have your coffee—excuse me, hot chocolate—and work on whatever you're doing. I can keep myself busy." He grabbed the remote and turned on the TV.

Noreen stared at him for a moment. He looked comfortable and content as if he'd meant every word. She sat down at her table then turned to her work, hiding a smile. Mr. Smith was definitely wrong. She wouldn't be going to bed alone.

# Chapter 13

Clyde Harris stubbed out his cigarette in a quick, definite motion before lighting another one. His recent call to Arlene bothered him, but not as much as the message he'd received. Someone didn't trust her and had let him know.

That annoyed him. He'd groomed Arlene well and chosen her with care. Her connection to Obsidian had been a plus. She was loyal and obedient. He'd even considered marriage. His wife, dead for years now, had been a great companion in both business and the bedroom and he had hoped to have Arlene fill the same position. With her sweet smile she could charm as well as his poor wife had. Although it would take a few more years to give Arlene the sophisticated polish his darling had.

He took a long drag of his cigarette and thought about his wife. He no longer felt any sorrow, but a deep regret. Her death had been unfortunate, but she'd forgotten the dangerous game they were playing. Mistakes were costly and she'd paid the ultimate price. He stared with pride down at the lights of the city below his apartment window. He remembered being a little boy growing up in Brooklyn. He hadn't had a view then because there hadn't been any windows. He, his brother and mother had lived in a damp basement apartment that belonged to a woman who made his mother wash and iron all the clothes for her large family in exchange for rent. He remembered having to go to sleep to the sound of the spinning washing machine that knocked against the wall, and how the dryer would turn the room into a sauna.

He'd been surrounded by ugliness: the chipping paint haphazardly applied to the concrete walls, the makeshift kitchen, frayed rugs and worn bedsheets. He'd stared up at the ceiling one day, vowing that he'd live better when he grew up. He knew he'd been meant for better things, like fine new clothes instead of leftovers from some rich person's closet that had either gotten stained or gone out of fashion.

He'd been meant for good food instead of the mush that came out of a can that his mother forced him to eat. He'd despised the woman. She'd had no aspirations and was a haggard, unattractive woman who didn't know how to dress or style her hair. He hadn't blamed his father for leaving her. He would have left her too and eventually did when he was fifteen and felt free to take charge of his own destiny. A destiny filled with beautiful things.

He'd soon learned that destiny was something one had to fight for. Hard work didn't equal great gain. He'd taken many jobs and none of them had gotten him even close to the lifestyle he deserved, so he did the only thing he knew would work.

He'd known the upper classes weren't going to let him in, so he'd forced his way in without them even suspecting it. He'd refined his manners, his clothes and his strategy. He'd made sure to mingle with people of influence and make connections that would prove beneficial in the future. That's when his dear wife, Elle, had entered his life and changed it. She'd grown up in a world he'd been on the outside of, and she'd let him in.

Together they'd created a business that still couldn't be rivaled. He looked around his stylish apartment, at the culmination of all his dreams. It was his sanctuary. He'd never invited anyone there. He had another residence he used for show, but this place was for him alone. But he knew he was getting older and couldn't keep going at the pace he had in the past. He wanted companionship and Arlene suited him. She was young and malleable and eager to please. He could teach her and mold her into anything he wanted.

He didn't want to believe the message. He knew she could be foolish sometimes, but not careless. He would have to find out the situation for himself.

The next day Michael and Noreen were inseparable as they tried out several of the cruise ship's many activities.

In the morning, Noreen made a bet with Michael that she could scale the onboard climbing wall. Unfortunately, she selected the most difficult challenge, and by the time she got to the top, she froze and had to have one of the crew help bring her down.

She hugged her rescuer in gratitude. "Will you marry me?"

He laughed as he released her safely back on the ground.

Michael came up behind her and rested a hand on her shoulder. "I could have rescued you."

She glared at him. "You were too busy laughing at me."

"I would have rescued you *after* I'd stopped laughing."

Noreen stuck her tongue out at him and marched off to change.

"I have a special place for us to have lunch," Michael said after they'd returned their climbing gear.

"Really? Where? Is it the Coco Lounge?" Noreen asked, thinking of the expensive restaurant on the ship.

He stopped in front of the elevators. "No, it's more exclusive."

"Then let's go."

He took out a bandana. "But you have to close your eyes."

"Why?"

"Because it's a surprise."

"If I wear that, people will look at me."

"You won't even notice. Do you trust me?"

Noreen thought about the great time they'd had on St. Barnaby. She'd taken a risk then, why not now? "Definitely."

"Good," he said then tied on the bandana and then waved his hand in front of her face. "No peeking."

"I won't."

Michael took Noreen's hand then led her into the elevator. They went up together in the elevator and then she followed him down a long hall. She heard a couple chatting and wind sweeping over a lounge chair and felt the warmth of the hot afternoon sun. Michael suddenly stopped and she heard a door open.

"Okay," he said. "Now you can look."

Noreen took off her blindfold and stared in amazement at Michael's grand suite, which had a large bouquet of red and white roses on the center table and a two-tier tray of delicious tarts and cookies off to the side. She sat down in an overstuffed side chair. "Oh, this is nice."

Michael closed the door behind him. "No, you're not supposed to sit there."

Noreen stared at him, confused. "Why not?"

He lifted her up in his arms and carried her over to the bed. "Because the last time you were here, you took care of me." He gently set her down. "Now it's my turn to take care of you." He took off her shoes.

Noreen grinned and got under the sheets, relishing the feel of the satin sheets and plush pillows. "Oh, this sounds like fun. The first time I was in here I'd wondered what it would be like to be in your bed." She pulled the sheets up to her chin. "Oooh, it feels so good." She stopped when she noticed him studying her. "What?"

He sat on the edge of the bed, a faint smile on his lips. "For a second I knew what you looked like as a little girl."

Noreen let the sheets fall and winked. "But I'm not a little girl anymore."

Michael's expression grew serious. "Do you know how old I am?"

She leaned forward. "Ask me if I care," she whispered against his lips before she kissed him. She drew back and rested her hands on her lap. "Now what comes next?"

Michael placed a hand against her neck, looking pensive. "Your fever has gone down."

Noreen frowned. "My fever?"

"Yes, you were running a fever when I found you on the beach."

She raised her brows. "You found me on the beach?"

He nodded. "Yes. You were unconscious and I brought you back here."

Noreen grinned, enjoying the game of make-believe. "So you rescued me."

"Yes, you were hesitant at first, but then I finally convinced you to let me help you."

"I'm sure it didn't take you long to convince me."

His jaw twitched. "Longer than I'd wanted."

"Next time I won't argue."

"Promise?"

"Of course," Noreen said, surprised he was so intense

when they were just pretending. She suddenly grabbed the front of her shirt. "Oh, no."

Michael started. "What?"

"I feel faint. I need some food."

He laughed and stood. "I'll get it for you." He arranged a bed tray then rested it on her lap.

Noreen stared down at several spicy crabcakes, asparagus and rice pilaf. "This looks wonderful. You didn't have to do all this. Mmm, it's delicious."

"I didn't cook it."

"I didn't think you did." She patted the space beside her. "There's enough room for both of us."

Michael sat on the bed and rested his arm behind her. "Eat up."

Noreen glanced at him, concerned. "Aren't you going to eat anything?"

He shook his head. "I'm not hungry."

"But I can't eat all this wonderful food while you just sit there." She scooped up some of the crabmeat then held it out to him. "Just take one bite."

He shook his head again, this time with a smile. "No, that's not how it works. I'm supposed to be taking care of you."

"We can take care of each other. Come on."

Michael stared at her for a long moment with the same sense of wonder he'd had when they'd first met, then he took a bite.

"Did you like it?"

"Yes, it's good." He gently stroked her cheek. "Now eat the rest for me. I'll eat something later." He turned away and flipped on the TV before she could argue. She sensed something was wrong, but couldn't decide what. He didn't seem in the mood to talk so Noreen ate in silence, stealing glances at his stoic profile. She wanted to tell him how much she loved him; that no one had thought to take care of her. She'd never had someone to rely on or to go to with her fears. But although she had so much to say, no words came to her and the silence continued to linger. When she was finished eating, Noreen leaned against him, wondering if he'd even realized she was there. Her uneasiness slipped away when his arm fell to her shoulders and he drew her closer to him.

To her relief, he agreed to share dessert with her and they enjoyed the tarts and cookies before Michael set their empty plates outside the door. He joined her back in bed, but although she was up to an amorous encounter, he just held her close. Noreen didn't ask any questions and soon drifted off into sleep.

In the evening, they decided to visit one of the night-spots. The cruise had fantastic entertainment, with a mix of large, pulsating spaces as well as smaller intimate venues, which kept the ship busy every night. Michael decided he wanted to take in one of the variety shows in the large amphitheater and the late-night comedy show. Noreen enjoyed herself, but sensed Michael was edgy. When she asked him, he told her he was fine.

"Do you have any plans for the holidays?" Michael asked her as they walked hand in hand along the deck. They enjoyed the starry moonlit sky above as a soft, salty breeze passed them, warm and fragrant.

"Not really."

"You won't be with Clyde?"

*Clyde.* She'd forgotten about him. She wished Michael would do the same. "I don't know. We haven't made plans."

"A friend of mine invited me over. He's in North Carolina."

"I see."

Michael stopped walking and looked at her. "You don't want me to come and visit, do you?"

"No, it's not that," Noreen said before she could stop herself. It was partly that, but also something more. The problem was once their time together was over, she'd be Noreen again. She squeezed his hand. "It's my sister."

"You don't think she'll like me?"

*She'll love you.* "Right now you'll be hard to explain." She moved her shoulders in an impatient manner as if to rid herself of the worry. "But let's not think about the future right now. I bought you something."

"When?"

"That's my secret." She rummaged in her handbag and pulled out a small teddy bear. "He's no Saint Christopher," she said, keeping her voice light in case he thought the gift was childish, "but he can keep you company."

Michael took the teddy bear and studied it for a long moment. He drew in his lips then looked at her. "Why does this feel like we're saying goodbye?"

Because she knew that they were. Tomorrow they would dock in St. Lagans and she would make the delivery. And she would have to come up with a good excuse not to be with him. She also knew that St. Lagans meant that their time together was coming to an end. After docking at the last island on the cruise, they would return to Miami and their separate lives.

"I don't know," she lied. "Do you like it?"

"Yes, I do," he said, but his hard gaze belied his soft words.

Noreen brushed her lips against his, unable to answer the questions in his eyes. "I'm glad," she said then took his hand and forced him to continue walking. She glanced up at the sky, wondering how she would be able to say goodbye.

Michael's sleep was restless. There had been nights after Jen's betrayal when he'd been unable to close his eyes without seeing her face. Tonight was one of those nights. He remembered the smile she'd given him before his world became a hazy blur. It was only later he realized she'd drugged him. "Gotcha," was the last thing she'd said. She'd been one of his major assignments. A housewife trapped in an unhappy marriage, who wanted to sell some items to raise enough money to leave her husband.

He'd later learned it was all a scam. He had met Jenelle Alvarez when she had introduced herself as a friend of Darren's deceased wife. Because of that connection, Michael hadn't put up any of his usual defenses. She was a beautiful, passionate woman whom Michael found extremely attractive, but he did not act on his attraction. Sleeping with married women, no matter how miserable their current relationship, was a taboo for him—although at times she made it difficult to resist because she offered herself in ways that would have made it very easy for him to break that taboo. However, he was eager to establish himself so he decided to focus on business.

The antiques she had wanted to sell consisted of several rare manuscripts and paintings. She provided him with all the provenance information, confirming the authenticity of the items, and he found several private buyers and a museum. He sold the items for a total of 1.3 million. Three months after the sales, Michael woke up from a night he couldn't remember with police at his door. One large piece, a rare sculpture by a renowned artist, had been reported stolen. Soon buyers began contacting him, complaining that the items were forgeries. By that time, Jen, along with her husband, had disappeared. Michael was to discover that her sad tale was just that. Her husband was a professional forger and con artist who ran a successful enterprise using blackmail, money laundering and more to make a living. He had created the documentation and worked with several skilled artists to create the items. Michael was able to trace the couple to an island, but without enough funds (to bribe officials) and because of the island's laws against extradition, Michael found himself having to settle with each of the buyers, using his own money and borrowing from Darren, who hired a top-notch attorney to defend Michael against some angry VIPs who had unwittingly purchased the forgeries.

Jen had been his biggest failure and his greatest teacher. She'd taught him how women worked and how to manipulate them. She'd helped to harden his heart to never trust—her face loomed in his dream beautiful, haughty and cold. Then it melted away and he saw Arlene with her arms stretched out to him and they made passionate love.

Soon Michael's body felt as if it could conquer the world. His body felt hard and aroused. He hadn't had a dream like this since he was sixteen. He vaguely knew he had to wake up or he was going to come right there in the bed and he didn't want to do that. He struggled to open his eyes, but he couldn't move, the wet tunnel of pleasure embracing his most sacred part keeping him paralyzed and he climaxed, releasing his seed, his entire body trembling from the power of it.

Then he felt the covers lift and Arlene peeked her head out. "You taste better than a lollipop."

"That was you?"

"I wanted you to relax."

Michael moaned then wrapped his arms around her. Her body was soft and warm. He held her close for more reasons than he could name. "I certainly will now," he mumbled then drifted into a contented sleep, still holding her.

More than five hours later, Noreen woke up and slipped out of bed, careful not to wake him. She looked at the clock and realized she had the perfect opportunity to slip off the boat and make the delivery and be back by lunch.

Noreen crept over to her dresser and promptly stumbled over his shoes. She picked up one shoe, resisting the urge to throw it at him. Why couldn't he just put them against the wall or in the closet instead of leaving them in the middle of the room? She glanced at him, relieved to see that he was still asleep. He was wonderful in so many other ways she could forgive him for this one flaw. Noreen picked up his shoes and put them out of the way then quickly changed. She then put the package to be delivered in her handbag.

Before leaving, Noreen went over to her table and grabbed a piece of paper out of her journal and wrote a brief message for Michael then left.

The day was overcast but that didn't deter anyone from visiting the island and enjoying the many activities scheduled. Once she'd disembarked, Noreen stood off to the side, looked around and saw no one waiting for her. She rested against a short post and checked her watch.

"Come with me," a familiar voice said.

Noreen looked up and saw Mr. Smith.

She shook her head. "I was told to wait here."

"It's only a few feet away. He doesn't want to be seen."

Noreen didn't understand the man's behavior. It seemed odd for the delivery of an antique ring. "No, he has to come to me."

Mr. Smith swore. "Listen, lady, do you want this to go through or not?"

"I'm not going anywhere with you. If the client wants the package, he has to come to me."

Mr. Smith sent her a look then said, "Don't move." And left. A few seconds later she saw a tall man approaching and she nearly collapsed.

"Clyde!"

He smiled, but it wasn't warm. "Arlene." He drew her closer and kissed her.

"What are you doing here?" she asked, rubbing her hands together so she wouldn't wipe her mouth.

"I thought I'd come and surprise you," he said in a smooth tone. He took her elbow and led her in the direction Mr. Smith had gone. "Now, let's go."

Noreen searched her mind, trying to make sense of everything. Something was terribly wrong. "What are you doing here?" she repeated, unable to think of anything else to say.

His pace was quick and determined. The bustle of the dock behind them soon grew distant. "I just told you."

Noreen licked her lips, fighting a sense of panic. There had to be a reason for this, but she couldn't understand what it was. As he led her down an isolated alley her uneasiness grew. "But if you were coming all this way, why didn't you make the delivery yourself?"

He sent her a sharp look as chilling as a snake's. "It's not like you to question me."

Noreen forced a weak smile. He was right. Arlene wouldn't worry. She'd be happy to see him. "I'm sorry, baby. I'm just so surprised."

"Of course you are." He suddenly stopped in a cove of trees where a large gray car was parked. The driver opened the door for them. Noreen hesitated. She might be able to outrun Clyde and Mr. Smith, but the driver, a bearded man in a crisp uniform, looked powerfully built and she felt his intense stare from behind his shaded glasses. No, he wouldn't let her get away. Noreen reluctantly got inside the car, holding back the questions that were filling her mind. What was Clyde really doing here? Where were they going? Would she get back to the ship in time?

Clyde said something to the driver then sat down beside her. Once the car began moving he said, "Do you have the package?"

"Yes, it's in my handbag."

He patted her on the knee. "Good girl. Once this is all over I'm going to treat you. I have the entire day planned."

Noreen forced a smile. "How wonderful." She glanced out the window at the unfamiliar landscape, trying to grab hold of her panic. After what seemed like an hour the car stopped.

The driver hurried over and opened Noreen's car door. She stepped out and saw an enormous, stately mansion jutting out over the sea. It was a magnificent structure that looked as if it had been carved out of the rock. The house was surrounded by a large iron fence and had a guard post at the front entrance. Whoever lived here, she thought, was very rich and liked his privacy. Noreen followed Clyde inside. The butler greeted the visitors and directed them to a large living room decorated with life-size ebony sculptures and original oil paintings. The owner either liked the finer things in life or wanted to appear to.

Before they could sit and enjoy their surroundings, a beefy man appeared, with beady eyes and a heavy gait, who seemed more suited to a wrestling ring than a mansion. Clyde walked over to him. The two men spoke in low voices before Clyde turned to her. "Give him the package."

Noreen took the package out of her handbag and handed it to the man, ignoring Clyde and the man's lack of civility. Obviously this was the client, Mr. Erickson.

He disappeared into a small room off to the side then came storming out. "Where is it?"

"What do you mean?" Clyde asked and took the package from him. He checked then glared at Noreen.

"Where is it?"

"You have it."

Clyde showed her the empty box.

Noreen stared, stunned. "It was there when I checked last night, I swear."

He slapped her across the face so hard that she saw stars. His voice dropped in volume. "I'm going to ask you again. Where is it?"

A cold knot formed in her stomach—a mingling of rage and fear. "I don't know what you're talking about."

"She's lying," Erickson said.

"She's not lying," the driver countered.

The two men turned and stared at him.

Clyde spoke first. "What?"

"She's not lying," he repeated. "She doesn't have it." He held up the ring. "I do."

"Who are you?" Clyde demanded.

"An old acquaintance," the driver said then removed his disguise. Within seconds the bearded driver turned into Michael.

# Chapter 14

Noreen gasped but no one paid attention to her.

"So we meet again," Clyde said with a sneer. "We have to stop doing that."

Erikson frowned. "What the devil is going on?" He pushed a button located on the wall. "Where's Smith?"

Michael absently rubbed his knuckles. "He's indisposed at the moment." He nodded to the button. "And you can keep ringing that, but no one is going to come. Now, here's what I want."

Clyde fumbled for something at his side then froze.

Michael held up a small gun and waved it as though Clyde had misplaced a toy. "Looking for this?"

Clyde swore then bent to reach for his leg. Michael cocked the gun and pointed it straight at him. "Please stand still. I don't want to kill you. There's a lady present."

Clyde grabbed Noreen and wrapped his arm around her neck. "A lady?" he sneered. "I wouldn't call her that." He saw Michael's grip on the gun waver and smiled. "Women are still your weakness." He put his lips near Noreen's ear and whispered. "Did you fall for him? I worked so hard to make sure you were loyal to me, but you still fell for him. Poor, stupid Arlene. You think your shipboard Romeo really wanted you? This was all a game. We both used you. You know why *I* needed you. He needed you to get to me. He's always traveling on cruise ships, wooing woman to get the info he needs. What's the name he's using now? Michael? Maurice? Matthew? I've lost track. But that doesn't matter because you're not his first. Jen fell for it too."

Noreen didn't move, both because she couldn't and didn't dare to.

"That's enough, Alvarez," Michael said. "It was clever of you to hide by using Clyde Harris, the name of one of your minions, but it didn't fool us for long."

Alvarez ignored him. "Did he tell you about Jen? She was my wife and a beautiful woman. But the most interesting part about her is how she died." He looked at Michael. "Would you like me to demonstrate? I am a businessman so I don't mind a little negotiation. You put down that gun and I won't break her neck." He stroked the side of Noreen's face. "She's so small, it won't be difficult."

Noreen knew she had to save herself. She came up with a daring plan she wasn't sure would work, but she didn't know of another option. Standing still so that Clyde could either strangle her or break her neck didn't seem like a good alternative. What she needed was a diversion. She caught Michael's eye then glanced down then back at him.

Michael pulled the trigger and shot the wall behind a large vase. Erickson screamed like a woman. "Stay still. Next time I won't miss." He returned his attention to Alvarez. "I'm also a businessman. I want to know where the stash is," Michael said.

His change of topic distracted Alvarez enough for Noreen to slip her hand into his pocket. She fought to keep her breathing even so he wouldn't suspect anything. She slipped her hand in and quickly pulled out his cigarette lighter. Working only from touch she flipped the top off and struck it. It didn't work.

She heard Michael talking but didn't understand what he was saying, desperate to get the lighter to work. She tried again and felt it come to life, then she held it up to his linen shirt. The smell of burning soon followed and she felt him stiffen.

"What's that smell?"

Michael nodded at him. "You."

He glanced down, stunned, and released Noreen to pat out his shirt. Michael rushed him and pinned him to the floor. "Where is the property?"

"I don't know what you're talking about."

Michael looked up at Erickson. "I'll give you the ring intact and you give me the location and we'll pretend we've never met. I know what's supposed to be inside the ring and I know where you can get more. Quickly."

Alvarez laughed although his face was pressed to the floor. "You can't believe him. He's a common thief who is in over his head."

"He's right. I'll just shoot the vase instead." He raised his gun.

"A barge on the other side of the island," Erickson blurted.

"Thank you," Michael said.

He made a quick motion with his hand and four island officers entered. He spoke to two of them in a low voice then to Erickson. "Take them to the site." He then addressed the two other officers and gestured to Alvarez. "Take him away."

"Don't think you've stopped me," Alvarez said.

Michael ignored him and walked over to Noreen. "Are you okay?"

Noreen hugged herself, unable to speak.

Alvarez snorted. "I should have known you'd try for a bigger fish. He'll drop you right where I left you."

"That's enough," Michael said.

"Did she tell you about the baby?" Alvarez asked as the officers cuffed him. He smiled maliciously when he saw the shock on Michael's face and the horror on Noreen's. "I saw the pregnancy test in your trash, baby. How far along are you? Do you think anyone will want you when you're carrying my child? I'm going to get out and I will get you."

His cold words sent a shiver of fear through her.

"Take him away," Michael said in disgust then turned to Noreen and again asked, "Are you all right?"

Noreen stared up at the man who was suddenly a stranger to her. "Who are you?"

"You know who I am."

Noreen shook her head. "No, I don't. He said that this is what you do. Not only are you a thief, but you use women to—"

Michael shook his head. "I'm an investigator and I'm everything I've told you. I'm just doing this job for a friend then I plan to go back to my ordinary life. I write travel articles. I've been doing this investigative work on and off for a long time. My cousin Undy saw I had a knack of charming people."

"Particularly women?" Noreen asked sourly.

"He taught me to use what talents I had to help people."

"He taught you well."

Michael paused, unsure if that was an insult or a compliment. "Yes, but I wasn't using them with you."

"Okay." Noreen turned to leave, not knowing where she would go, but just wanting to get away from him.

Michael jumped in front of her. "I'm sorry I couldn't tell you anything, but Erickson just gave me the location where Alvarez has been stashing his stolen antiques, which is the information I was after."

"So you sought me out to get to Clyde, uh, Alvarez."

"At first yes, but—"

"And this was all a game…"

"No, I mean, it started out just being a job but when I realized you were in danger I wanted to protect you. When I saw what you had in your suitcase—"

"You went through my things?"

"I had to if I was going to keep you safe. Do you know what was inside that ring you were carrying? It's a new designer drug that St. Lagans has banned. His last two carriers ended up in prison. When I discovered what was really going on and why The Shark was following you—"

"The Shark?"

"Yes, that's the nickname of the man who grabbed you on the dance floor. He's a dangerous man and got that nickname because people around him usually end up dead. Alvarez sometimes uses him to monitor high-risk situations. Erickson doesn't like anyone close to him to handle certain transactions, which is why Alvarez uses unsuspecting go-betweens who will be linked to whatever false identity he's using. When I discovered what I suspected was going on, I contacted Darren, my client, and we came up with a plan to trick Alvarez into coming here, by having someone send him a message that you couldn't be trusted.

"He's eluded police for so long and I wanted it to end. My only assignment was to get the property location and find 'Harris,' but when I saw Erickson's man I knew something more was going on.

"I discovered that Alvarez had killed Harris and taken over his business and identity. I had to do my job no matter what. This is my last assignment and a favor for a friend. I didn't want it to end with losing a woman like you."

He sighed fiercely. "Arlene, I've never felt this way for someone. I know you're scared but I know you feel it too, and it's real and we can't let it go. I don't want you to worry about anything. I'm not worried about the baby. I knew there was something that tied you to him and now I know what it is. I've never had a family and I wouldn't mind being a dad, just the way Undy was to me. Whatever is part of you is part of me."

Noreen opened her mouth, but no words emerged. It was all a charade. A lie. Noreen couldn't focus on his explanation although it made sense. He'd saved her life. Who knew what would have happened to her if Michael hadn't been there. He'd lied to her, but she'd lied to him. All this time they'd both been wearing masks, both pretending to be someone else. Noreen didn't realize she was crying until Michael brushed a tear away. "I know it's a lot to take in."

"Sir!" an officer called out to him.

"I'll be right with you," he said, his gaze never leaving Noreen's face. "There are several things I have to take care of first. There's a taxi outside that will take you back to the ship. Angel, I'm sorry, but—"

"No, don't apologize. I think it's better we remember everything as it was. It was a good time and now it's over. Goodbye, Michael," Noreen said then ran outside.

When Michael returned to the ship he went straight to Arlene's cabin and knocked.

"She's gone," Joy said from behind him.

He turned to her. "What do you mean 'she's gone'?"

"She cleared her room and took a plane to the mainland."

"And you didn't stop her?"

Joy raised a mocking eyebrow.

Michael swore fiercely. "Sorry, it's not your fault." He went to the railing and watched as the ship left the dock. It was too late for him to go after her. She'd once called him a pirate and she was right. But he'd found a treasure he was not going to stop looking for.

# Chapter 15

*North Carolina, two months later*

A chill December wind knocked bare branches together as snow drifted past a festively dressed house where fresh evergreen garlands swept from window to window and hung over the front door. A large wreath above the door and side windows offered a traditional welcome, while a bundle of greenery and a crisp, red bow trimmed the lamppost.

Inside the foyer a large oval table sat in the center of the entry hall, featuring fresh fruits and flowers of the season. Noreen stood by the window in the family room, in awe of the room's floor-to-ceiling windows and the ten-foot Christmas tree that was expertly decorated, providing the perfect background for the festive occasion.

Her friend Suzanne's parties were always spectacular affairs, but her holiday parties were exceptional. Everyone in town and abroad wanted to get an invitation. Garlands hung over the grand banister and fireplace. The scent of gingerbread cookies and peppermint candy filled the air, and large scented wax candles sat in various locations throughout the house. In the formal living room, sparkling gold decorations and white lights provided a cheery welcome for visitors. Creamy white poinsettias and grapevine trees wrapped with tiny fairy-like lights filled the space beside the staircase.

Waiters in tuxedos slipped soundlessly through the crowd with trays of hors d'oeuvres, including smoked salmon canapés, ham-and-cranberry-cream-cheese sandwiches, black-bean tartlets and curried chicken turnovers. The dinner for the evening consisted of endive salad with pancetta, pecan-crusted rack of lamb, roasted vegetables and smoked mozzarella bread puddings and, for dessert, pear frangipane tarts were served on elegant custom-designed Christmas china.

People laughed and talked, clearly enjoying themselves. Noreen wished she could too.

"What happened?" a female voice said behind her.

Noreen spun around and looked at Claudia, whose festive outfit could rival a Christmas tree.

"What do you mean?"

"Your revised manuscript is wonderful. Did you send it in to your editor?"

"Yes. Right after you and Suzanne had given me your feedback."

"Great, now back to my question. What happened?"

"Why do you keep asking me that?"

Suzanne joined them. "Because your story was amazing. I'm jealous. How did you come up with such a delicious hero?"

"Thank you for your compliment," Noreen said primly, keeping her emotions in check. "But this is a party. I really don't want to talk shop."

"I can't help it," Claudia said. "I need answers."

Noreen shrugged. "I just made a few revisions."

Claudia shook her head, unconvinced. "Approximately three months ago I read a manuscript that almost put me to sleep. Then I get your newly improved story and I couldn't fall asleep for two days thinking about the characters. Their love is so strong I nearly wept and I'm not a mushy romantic. An emotional power pulsed from every word. Those love letters were inspired." She tapped her chin. "So what happened?"

"I told you," Noreen responded with irritation. "I just decided to revise it based on your suggestions." She couldn't tell them the truth about the cruise and definitely not about Michael. He was an experience that no one would know about.

"You're lying."

"Leave her alone," Suzanne said. "Your editor is going to love it, and your fans will even more."

Noreen smiled. "Thank you."

"But we're worried about you."

Her smile fell. "Worried about me?"

"Yes, you don't seem like yourself."

Claudia nodded. "You're more uptight than usual."

"I'm not uptight."

Suzanne shook her head. "She phrased that wrong. You seem preoccupied." Her friend sighed, as if trying to find the right words. "You've just written a wonderful manuscript, and it's the holidays and you're here with us, but you don't seem happy."

Noreen stared at her friends, unable to respond. She wasn't happy and she'd stopped believing in the holiday spirit. She didn't know when, but every year the magic seemed to fade away until it was gone. All the gaiety around her didn't penetrate the coldness in her heart. She'd thought she'd never feel numb again and she didn't. After leaving Michael she felt an aching emptiness. She knew she'd never see him again and for a time she'd let the memory of him warm her, but as days turned to months, thoughts of him and why she'd left without an explanation were painful. She knew how much risk he'd taken asking her to run away with him and she didn't want to think about how her desertion may have hurt him. She sometimes wondered what would have happened if she'd said yes. But she was too practical to think about it for long.

Had he forgotten about her? Had he taken another case? But the answers didn't matter. She had to forget him.

"It's been a stressful time," she said vaguely.

Claudia nudged her with her elbow. "Well, we're here if you need us."

"Yes," Suzanne agreed. "And I think—" She stopped and looked down and saw her seven-year-old son, Luke, tugging on her skirt. Suzanne smiled down at him. "Well, this is a surprise."

Noreen was surprised to see him too. Luke was very shy and usually stayed in his room. "Hello, Miss Claudia and Miss Noreen," he said very solemnly.

Noreen smiled at him and Claudia said, "Cute and has manners." She bent down to his level. "Will you run off with me?"

He lowered his eyes and giggled.

Suzanne straightened his tie. "What do want, honey?"

"I can't find Harmon." Harmon was his pet frog.

Suzanne froze. "What?"

Her husband, Rick, joined them with his hands in his pockets and an amused expression on his face. "I guess he's already told you."

Suzanne glanced at him then Luke. "Go back to your room and look *really* hard."

The little boy nodded and ran away.

Suzanne turned to Rick, careful to keep her voice composed. "Where's your mother?"

"Looking for the—"

Suzanne covered his mouth. "Don't say it," she hissed, looking around. "I don't want anyone to overhear you."

He removed her hand. "Okay."

"I don't believe this. The first holiday party in our new house and there's a missing…thing…somewhere."

Rick affectionately rubbed Suzanne's shoulders. "Relax, no one has screamed yet."

"Excuse us," Suzanne said to her friends and took Rick's hand.

"Sorry, ladies," he said and waved at Claudia and Noreen as Suzanne dragged him away.

"Poor Suzanne," Noreen said.

"Don't feel sorry for her. Rick can handle any mishaps." She watched Rick steal a kiss under the mistletoe. Suzanne shoved him away, but he only laughed. "They're so in love. You can feel it all the way over here. If every woman were as well-adjusted as she is, I'd be out of a job. Thank God for women like us."

"Like us?"

"Yes, happily single."

"Right," Noreen said in a flat voice.

Claudia sent her a sharp glance. "Or has that changed?"

"No," she said quickly. "Nothing's changed."

Of course that was a lie. Everything about her life had changed since she'd returned.

Claudia tugged on her earring. "I know we may not agree on everything, but you know that I love you and I want you to be happy."

"I know."

She lowered her voice in concern. "Is anything wrong?"

"I just have a lot to think about." Such as dealing with her sister, an ex who reported her to the courts because she'd missed an alimony payment and sleepless nights because of a man she couldn't stop thinking about. "But I came to this party to get away from all that."

"Fair enough. Just remember one thing. Heartbreak is nothing to be ashamed of. Sometimes pain reminds us that we're alive." She walked away.

* * *

Noreen remembered Claudia's words more than a week later as she sat in her family room, creating a new story on her laptop.

"You work too hard," Arlene complained, coming into the family room with a large cardboard box.

Noreen looked up and watched as Arlene set the box down. When she stood the gentle swell of her belly was starting to show through her red spandex top. She was nearly five months along now and glowing with good health and in high spirits, which was a nice change from months ago. After the incident in St. Lagans, Noreen had returned to the ship, gathered her things from her cabin then gone straight to the airport and flown out. She'd called her sister the moment she'd touched down and they'd met at Noreen's house.

"I have something to tell you," Noreen said as they sat in her kitchen.

"Me first," Arlene said eagerly. "I'm pregnant."

Noreen's face fell. "I was afraid of that."

"Why? I know it wasn't planned but Clyde will take care of me."

She shook her head. "No, he won't."

"I know you don't like him, but—"

Noreen took her hand. "Arlene. I have a few things to tell you." She told her sister all about what happened in St. Lagans, carefully leaving out any mention of Michael. Telling her sister that the man she'd loved was really named Alvarez and was an accused murderer and smuggler was enough.

Arlene stared at Noreen, dumbfounded, then touched her stomach and gulped ominously. "I think I'm going to be sick." She covered her mouth then raced over to the sink.

After being violently ill, Arlene collapsed to the ground in tears. "How could I have been so wrong about him? I loved him. I was certain he was the one."

"Come on," Noreen said, helping her sister to her feet.

"I was so happy, Sis," she sobbed. "I thought we might get married. I'd already imagined what our wedding would be like."

Noreen led her sister to a guest bedroom. "I know." She helped her sister into the bed then tucked her in.

"What am I going to do? Now I have no job and no place to go. He paid for the apartment. I can't afford it now."

"You know you can stay here."

She sniffed and wiped her eyes. "I don't want to be a burden."

"Just go to sleep," Noreen said in a soothing tone as if lulling a child. "I'll take care of you."

And that had been all the assurance Arlene needed. She soon acted as if she had no cares in the world. She moved in with Noreen and only occasionally looked for work. Anytime Noreen asked if she would think of adoption, Arlene brushed her away. "You worry too much. I have plenty of time to think it over."

Although Arlene didn't like to talk about her impending motherhood, she enjoyed being pregnant. She wore the tightest tops she could to show off her small baby bump.

"Not all women look as good as me," Arlene said as they walked in a mall that was getting decorated for the holiday season. "My stomach is so symmetrical."

"You hardly show and I still think you should dress a bit more mature."

"Some men find pregnant women sexy."

Noreen sent her sister a sharp look. "You shouldn't be thinking about men right now."

"Why not? I may be pregnant, but I still have needs."

And for three weeks Arlene got her needs met from a gangly man Noreen only knew as Tyrone. But that relationship ended when he decided to spend Thanksgiving with his family and reconciled with his third ex-wife. Fortunately, Arlene bounced back from the rejection and immediately started on a new project: Christmas.

"It's four days before Christmas and you haven't decorated," Arlene said.

"I'm not celebrating this year."

"But you have to."

"No, I don't."

"Noreen!"

"What? I went to Suzanne's party. That's all the holiday cheer I need. If you wanted some you should have come too."

Arlene pulled her face into a pout. "It's not the same."

"I'm not decorating, but I bought you a gift if that's what you're worried about."

"That's not enough."

"It will have to be," Noreen said, ending the discussion.

That had been yesterday; evidently Arlene hadn't dropped the subject.

Noreen frowned as she looked at the box. "What is that?"

"Decorations. I thought it was time we decorated the place for the holidays. I feel in the mood to celebrate. Unfortunately, you don't have many ornaments. We're going to have to buy some."

"You just want an excuse to shop. I have plenty of things in the garage. I'll get them later."

Arlene collapsed on the couch and her top inched up. Arlene yanked it down. "I think this top has shrunk," she grumbled.

Noreen closed her laptop and set it aside. "No, your stomach has gotten bigger."

Her sister frowned. "It's starting not to be as much fun. It's getting uncomfortable."

"Stop complaining. Just wait until you're eight months along." Noreen stood and kissed her sister on the forehead. "You're still beautiful."

She smiled then her smile slowly fell. "Tyrone said—"

Noreen returned to her place on the couch. "I don't care."

"Do you think I'll ever meet him?"

"I doubt it. He's moved to Georgia."

Arlene shook her head. "No, not Tyrone. Him. The One. The man for me. A man who is caring and funny and sexy. Does a man like that even exist?"

Noreen thought about Michael. "Yes. Now don't get maudlin and go change your top unless you want to hold that one down all day."

Arlene stood and lowered her gaze, absently stroking the slight curve of her belly. "Will you be angry if I keep it?" She looked at Noreen, her eyes glistening with tears. "It would be nice to have something in my life that won't leave me."

Noreen stood and hugged her. "No, I won't be angry. I'm here for you."

"Do you think I'll make a good mother?"

Noreen knew her sister would make an unconventional mother, but she'd be loving and gentle. "Yes, and I'll make a fabulous aunt, but you need to realize that it's going to be a lot of responsibility."

"I know. I've thought about it a lot."

"Good. Then I'll support whatever decision you make."

"Really?" she said with surprise.

"Yes, except one."

"What?"

Noreen tugged on her sister's top as it kept inching upward. "Your decision to wear this. Please go and change."

Arlene left. Noreen watched her go then sank back into her chair, wishing she could make everything right for her sister. She wished the right man would come along and take care of her. Arlene was a fun and caring companion who would make any man a good wife. She needed someone strong and kind. Noreen thought about Michael. She missed him. Not just being in his arms, but his smile, his teasing eyes and how he'd listen to her stories and would make her feel wonderful.

She still loved him. She wished she didn't, but she did. She believed that he had cared for her during those few days. She'd been married to a liar and grown up with one, so she knew Michael had been sincere or maybe she just wanted to believe him. She wondered what he was doing now. Did he ever think of her? She sighed. Even if he did, it wouldn't be her, it would be "Arlene." She reached up and clasped the necklace she still wore around her neck.

A few minutes later, Arlene came back into the room wearing a more appropriate top. "I'm starving."

"You're always starving."

Arlene affectionately patted her stomach. "I'm eating for two, remember?"

"You act like you're eating for five. My grocery budget has tripled."

"Are you sure you don't mind me being here?"

"Arlene, I was teasing."

She sighed. "I know. I guess I just wish everything had turned out differently."

*Me too.* Noreen forced a smile. "I'm the one who's supposed to worry, not you. I've always taken care of things, haven't I?"

She nodded.

"So relax. I'll handle things."

Arlene's eyes lit up. "Will you help me decorate?"

Noreen rolled her eyes. "I'm busy."

"Please. Just this once."

Noreen reluctantly stood, knowing how the argument would eventually end. "Okay. I'll get the other boxes."

"Great! I'll be right back."

"Where are you going?"

"The kitchen is almost bare. I'm going grocery shopping. It's nice to have plenty of food in the house. You never know who might drop by."

"What do you mean?"

"It's the holidays, so people may want to visit. Do you want anything?" she added before Noreen could say anything.

"No," Noreen said, suddenly suspicious. "But what—"

"'Bye!" Arlene grabbed her car keys then left.

Noreen looked around her expertly decorated family room. She hadn't celebrated the holidays since her divorce, but this year would be different. If it made her sister happy, it would be worth the hassle. She pulled on her boots, a long wool coat and a pair of gloves and went out to her garage. She opened the door and stared at the orderly boxes stacked on top of each other, looking specifically for the ones labeled *Christmas*. After nearly twenty minutes she found them and started to pull them down.

"Noreen Webster?"

She spun around at the sound of the familiar voice. She froze when she saw the source of it. "Yes?"

"Hi, I'm Michael Vaughn."

# Chapter 16

Noreen hastily put down the small box of items she was holding before she dropped it. She couldn't breathe. What was he doing here?

Michael took a step forward, flashing his trademark smile. "Sorry, I didn't mean to scare you." He took another step forward. "It's amazing. Sorry to stare, but the resemblance is remarkable."

Noreen found her voice. "How can I help you?"

"Um...as I said my name is Michael Vaughn." He held out his hand and she briefly shook it, thankful they both wore gloves.

"Obviously you already know who I am."

"Yes, your sister told me about you, but I don't know if your sister told *you* about *me*."

"She did." He looked relieved. "And after all that she told me, I'm curious why you're here."

"I wish I'd come sooner," he said with chagrin, "but I had some business to take care of and then my cousin Undy got sick."

"I'm sorry," she said with more feeling than she'd meant to show. Noreen wouldn't know what his cousin meant to him.

"Thank you. Things were left unsettled between your sister and me and I want to fix that."

"Well, she's not here right now."

"That's okay, because I really want to speak to you first."

"Me?" Noreen's voice cracked.

"Yes. Do you have some time?"

She looked at her garage in dismay. Why did he want to talk?

"I won't get in your way. I noticed you were moving things. Can I give you a hand?"

Noreen pointed. "If you could grab that box over there, it would help." She picked up a medium-size box then went inside and set it down in the family room, next to the one Arlene had brought in. She briefly held her forehead and closed her eyes, trying to gain her composure. She needed to breathe. Relax. Just be herself. She was Noreen. She could handle anything.

Michael followed close behind and set another box down next to hers. He stood to his full height and looked wonderful but Noreen knew she had to treat him like a stranger.

She held out her hand then wiggled her fingers as

though impatient so he wouldn't notice it shaking. "Let me take your coat."

He handed it to her and looked around. "Nice place you have here. It's not what I expected."

No, it wouldn't be. Arlene's tastes were different.

"Your sister told me about you and I pictured how your place would be. It's better than I imagined," Michael continued. "It's warm and comfortable, like a true home."

"Thank you." Noreen escaped into the hallway and opened her coat closet and started to hang up his coat then she stopped. She held it close, for a moment, hugging the coat to her the way she wished she could hug him and tell him how much she'd missed him. Tears gathered in her eyes as she inhaled the fresh, cool scent of him and the winter air that clung to it. She took a deep steadying breath and composed herself and hung up his coat. She also removed hers and headed toward the living room then remembered her necklace and hastily tucked it under her shirt before entering the room.

She found Michael holding up a holiday ornament. "So you're decorating for Christmas?"

"Yes, that's Arlene's idea."

He smiled and set the ornament down. "She knows how to liven up a room."

Noreen pasted on a smile. "Always." She gestured to the couch, feeling like a robot. "Please take a seat."

Michael sat down, making himself comfortable. "How is she?"

"The first few weeks were hard but she's getting better."

"And she's healthy?"

"Yes, she's due in April." Noreen rubbed her hands. "Would you like anything to drink or eat?" When he didn't reply, she snapped her fingers in front of him.

He blinked. "What?"

"You're staring again."

Michael shook his head. "I'm sorry, it's just so amazing. Except for the glasses you look exactly the same."

Noreen folded her arms, uncomfortable by his scrutiny. "Yes, I suppose if you ignore the glasses, the clothes, the career, the house and her vivacious personality, my sister and I are *exactly* the same."

"Ouch," he said with good humor. "I guess I deserve that."

"I didn't mean to be rude."

He grinned. "Somehow I doubt that, but you made your point. You're two different women." He leaned forward. "Noreen, I won't waste your time. I want to ask your opinion."

"Go on."

"I'll come out and say it. I came to you because you and your sister are close and I know you'd know what she needs. I want to ask your sister to marry me. Do you think it's too soon?"

He wanted to marry her? Noreen's heart filled with joy then shattered when she remembered he was referring to Arlene. She looked at him, unable to form any words.

She heard the front door slam shut. "I'm back," Arlene called out. "I bet you were afraid I'd buy out the store." Arlene came into the room, carrying several grocery bags.

Michael jumped to his feet. "Hello, Angel. You look more beautiful than I remember."

Arlene stared at him. "What?"

Noreen rushed over to her, grabbed some bags and took her arm. "Excuse us." She pushed her sister into the kitchen.

"Who's that? He's gorgeous. Not in the regular way, but in that I-get-what-I-want-and-I-want-you way."

"His name is Michael Vaughn and there are a few things I forgot to tell you about my trip. We had an affair and he really likes you."

Arlene grinned. "Some sisters pick up souvenirs when they travel. My sister brings me back a man." Arlene put her bags down and headed out the door. "I need to get another look at him."

Noreen seized her arm. "He calls you Angel because you helped him after he got hit by a car."

Arlene tapped her chin. "That's a cute nickname. I like it."

"This is serious."

"And I'm seriously listening. Tell me what else I need to know."

Noreen gave her sister a quick summary of key information so that Arlene could bluff her way through.

Arlene nodded, processing everything. "Does he have money?"

"Yes."

"Even better." Arlene patted her sister's cheek. "Don't

worry, I know how to play this," she said then started to leave.

"Wait!"

"What?"

Noreen took off the necklace Michael had given her and placed it around Arlene's neck. "You have to wear this. He gave it to me…um, you, and it's important to him. He got it from his mother."

Arlene frowned and held the medal in her palm. "It's kind of ugly."

"That doesn't matter," Noreen said in a tight voice. "Now let's go before he gets suspicious."

Arlene calmly walked into the family room where Michael stood studying a picture of them as little girls. He turned when he heard them enter. "I didn't think I'd ever see you again," she said with feeling.

"I'm sorry I couldn't come sooner." He walked over to her. "I wanted to but so many things happened. I thought about you every day." His voice lowered. "You're just as I remembered you."

"Except a little bigger."

"To me you're always the perfect size." His gaze fell to the necklace. "You kept it." Before she could answer, he drew her close and kissed her.

Noreen turned away, feeling her insides shrivel. She was about to disappear into the kitchen when Arlene said, "Why don't you stay for dinner?"

"No, I'm sure he has lots to do," Noreen said.

"I'd like that," Michael replied at the same time.

They looked at each other and laughed awkwardly.

"I'm sorry," they said simultaneously.

Michael gestured to her. "You go first."

"I have a lot of work to do. Why don't you two go out? There's that restaurant—"

Arlene shook her head. "No, we're staying right here to keep you from working to death." She turned to Michael. "She works all the time. I have to drag her away, but she's been so good to me."

"I want to spend time with you, but only if that's okay with Noreen." He shifted his gaze to Noreen.

Arlene stood behind him and mouthed "Say yes."

At that moment Noreen hated her sister. "Of course." Noreen took a step back. "Are there more bags in the car?"

"Just one."

Michael released Arlene. "I can—"

"I'll get it," Noreen interrupted. She left and opened the trunk of her car, wishing she could just drive away. She was already in her sister's shadow. Now her special secret was over. At least before she could pretend that he'd cared for her, but now reality was staring her in the face. He treated her just like all the rest. There was no look of interest, no look of anticipated fun. But how could she have expected anything else? He was loyal. Noreen sighed, defeated. Why couldn't he have stayed away? Then their dream affair would have lasted forever.

She returned to the house and found Arlene alone. "Where's Michael?"

"Getting more boxes from the garage. He said he'll help me decorate. Oh, Noreen, he's wonderful. He's even better than wonderful. He's The One. He said he has a place for us on an island." Arlene ran up and hugged her. "After Clyde and Tyrone I can't believe I could be this lucky. I won't have to live off you. He'll take care of me." She patted her stomach. "And little me. This is the best Christmas ever. And it gets better."

Noreen's stomach clenched from impending doom. "How?"

"He has a friend."

"So?"

"So Michael asked me if he could invite him to join us for dinner because otherwise his friend would be alone. He said his friend's a really nice guy and I thought about you. His name is…" She squinted in thought. "It starts with a *D*. Derek or Derwin—"

"It's Durren," Michael corrected coming in to place two large boxes down. "I came to spend the holidays with him. He lost his wife a few years ago and I couldn't have a nice home-cooked meal while he's left alone with a TV dinner. That just doesn't seem fair. I hope you don't mind."

"No," Noreen said in a neutral tone, determined not to betray her feelings. "It's the season of giving. The more the merrier. Let me go get dinner started."

"Could we have fish cakes, Angel? I've been dreaming about yours for weeks."

Arlene frowned. "What?"

"I'll make them," Noreen said quickly. "Arlene's had a long day. I'm sure she'll make them for you another time. Let me go and see what I can throw together."

Noreen rushed into the kitchen and started gathering the necessary items for dinner. So much for the Chinese takeout she'd planned for today. She had to find something. She wanted to hate them both. Feelings of anger would stop her from wanting to cry. She knew Michael cared about Arlene and would take care of her and Arlene needed someone like him, especially now. And she knew her sister would easily fall in love with him, if she hadn't already. Now she wouldn't have to worry about her sister picking up another jerk.

As Michael had told her on the island, Arlene lived romance while Noreen just wrote about it. And her sister deserved a happy ending. It was perfect. They belonged together.

But no matter how much she tried to rationalize what was happening, that didn't stop their laughter from sounding like a knife against glass. The thought of them together made her heart ache. She felt wicked and selfish. Her misery grew when she heard Christmas music coming from her stereo and heard them singing along, their voices blending in perfect harmony.

Noreen listened to the music and groaned. She'd never been a big fan of Christmas and now she hated it. She suddenly felt as if the ghost of Jacob Marley would come and haunt her. Scrooge had nothing on her. How could she think anything but good for her sister? Why couldn't she genuinely want the two of them to be happy? She knew the reason, but didn't want to answer herself.

Moments later, she heard the doorbell ring and Arlene screamed, "Daddy!"

Noreen swore. Just what she didn't need. An unwanted

father-and-daughter reunion. She hadn't seen her father in nearly a year. She glanced at the ceiling, her words a fervent plea. "Kill me now."

## Chapter 17

"I just met Arlene's new man," Vince Webster said, entering the kitchen. He was a striking man with white hair and dark eyes. "Your sister is glowing."

"You surprise me," Noreen said sarcastically. "Now you'll tell me that ice is cold."

"Hello, Noreen," he said with a formal tone.

"Hello, Dad," she replied in equal measure.

"How are you doing?"

"Fine."

He shifted then cleared his throat. "She invited me over for dinner, but she obviously didn't tell you."

"I don't care. I'm making plenty of food. Right now I'm not quite sure what I'm making, but I'm sure it will be enough."

"Careful you don't cut yourself," he said, watching her quickly chop several green peppers.

"I will."

He glanced around the kitchen then looked at her. "It's good to see you."

"I'll be out with snacks soon," she said, hoping he'd get the hint and leave her alone. "Do you want anything to drink?"

Her father hesitated then sighed and said, "No," before leaving.

Noreen filled several small glass bowls with nuts and crackers and placed them on the coffee table out in the family room. "Nibble on these until dinner is ready."

"Come and help us," Arlene said as she placed an ornament on the tree.

"I have enough to do in the kitchen." Noreen returned to the kitchen before her sister could protest. She had to stay away from them and keep busy so that she wouldn't think.

As she checked the roasting chicken in the oven, she heard the doorbell ring again and went into the hallway to answer it. She saw Michael heading for the door.

"It's probably Darren," he said when he saw her. "I'll get it."

Noreen pushed past him, annoyed with how comfortable he'd made himself in her house. "That's okay, I'll get it." She opened the door ready to hate her new guest, and at first she did when she noticed the attractive older man dressed in an expensive Italian coat and cashmere scarf, but then she looked into his soft brown eyes and her heart softened. This man was genuine. She opened the door wider and offered him a smile. "You must be Darren. I'm Noreen."

"Thanks for having me," he said, stepping inside and taking off his coat.

"It's a pleasure." She opened the closet and hung up his coat.

"So you made it," Michael said, patting his friend on the back.

Darren smiled. "Yes, no thanks to your directions."

Michael laughed. "I was hoping you'd get lost so I could keep these two beautiful women all to myself."

Noreen turned to him sharply, but he was already leading Darren into the family room. *Two beautiful women?* Had he really said that? He had to be joking.

She shook her head and returned to the kitchen to make a salad. She ripped up the lettuce with pleasure.

"Are you angry?" Arlene asked, creeping into the kitchen like a child going to the principal's office.

Noreen turned to her. "You should have told me you had invited Dad."

"I knew you'd say no, and I want you two to get on. I thought a nice family dinner was in order. It's the holidays. I didn't know Michael would show up too. But it's all working out great. They like each other."

"Good."

"So you're not mad?"

*I'm furious.* "No."

"Oh, and isn't Darren cute? You just want to hug him."

A reluctant smile touched Noreen's lips. "Yes," she admitted.

Arlene kissed her sister on the cheek. "Thanks for everything. Could we get more nibbles?" She handed Noreen the empty bowls.

Noreen filled them.

Arlene took them from her and looped her arm through hers. "Come and see what we've done." She dragged Noreen into the family room.

"It looks great," Noreen said, admiring the tree and other decorations.

"Sit down and watch us turn on the lights," Arlene urged her.

"I really don't—"

Michael's voice cut through her protest. "Sit down."

She stared at him, surprised by his command.

"Please," Darren said in a softer tone.

Noreen shifted her gaze to him and slowly sank into a nearby love seat, biting back what she really wanted to say.

Arlene smiled and nodded at her father. "Okay, plug it in."

He did and all the lights came on.

"Beautiful," Noreen said, jumping to her feet.

Arlene's smile fell. "Where are you going?"

"If you want to eat dinner, I'd better be cooking."

"It doesn't usually take you that long."

"I don't usually cook for five."

"Make a large pizza or something then."

Noreen's lips thinned. "A pizza? Why not hot dogs and soda? Silly me, I should have thought of that before I started roasting a chicken."

"I didn't expect you to."

"We could order in if you want," Michael said.

"And waste the food I've already started?"

Michael narrowed his eyes. "We didn't ask you to make a feast."

"No, I guess I shouldn't have made anything."

"I didn't mean—"

Darren cut in. "We're really grateful for all that you're doing," he said, his smooth, deep voice calming the argument before it could escalate. "Don't let us bother you."

Noreen cooled her temper. "Thank you." She left and sighed with relief when she reached the safety of the kitchen. She cut the potatoes and put them in a bowl and began to mash them.

"You're a violent masher," a male voice said.

She ignored him and mashed harder, wishing she could do the same to the desire welling up inside her.

"Dinner smells good," he added.

She turned, recognizing the kind voice. "I'm sorry, Darren, I thought you were—"

"Michael?"

She nodded, ashamed.

"Forgive him. He's used to being in control of situations."

"I noticed."

"I think there are a few things about him that you should know. Your sister really is in good hands, but that's just my opinion and you don't know me."

"But I already like you."

His face lit up with a smile. "That's good to know." He rolled up his sleeves and headed to the sink.

"What are you doing?"

"Helping you wash up. You're going to have enough dishes after dinner. You might as well start clean." Darren filled the sink before Noreen could protest. "You can trust me. I used to help my wife in the kitchen all the time. Sometimes I'd help with the cooking." A soft look touched his face as he remembered her. "She'd—" He stopped.

"Go on," Noreen gently urged him.

"She'd find new recipes and we'd cook them together. I'd wash and she'd chop." He sighed. "They were good times."

Noreen lightly stroked his arm, touched by his love for his wife. "I'm sorry for your loss." She laughed bitterly. "I could never get my ex-husband into the kitchen."

"Then he was a stupid man because I would have come up with any excuse to be with the woman I love." He placed a pot in the dish rack nearby. "I know times like this are hard. It seems more memories come during the holidays than at any other time in the year."

"Yes," Noreen said, relieved to meet someone who understood.

"But you can't live in the past. I loved my wife, but that doesn't mean I won't ever love again. She wouldn't want that for me and loving someone is too precious to ignore."

"You mean you would get married again?"

"Definitely." He hesitated. "I don't know you very well, but from what Michael has told me about your sister, I know she hasn't had luck meeting good men. I want you to know that your sister is safe. Michael is one of the best men I know."

"You don't have to defend him to me," Noreen said quickly, not wanting to hear anything more about him.

"I think I do, especially after how he talked to you before. It was out of character for him. He's not usually that abrupt but I think you make him nervous."

"Me?"

"Yes. See he was basically raised by his cousin Undy—"

"I know, my sister told me about that."

"Did she tell you that he was a brute?"

"What? No, I thought—I mean she said that he loved him. Idolized him."

Darren nodded grimly. "Yes, he does for all the wrong reasons. Michael talks about him as if he's some savior because Michael is loyal and family means a lot to him, but his cousin used him. He started him working at fifteen and Michael didn't finish college because his cousin worked him so much he was too tired to focus on his studies.

"Undy hid the letters Michael's father sent to him wanting him to come and visit. He's mellowed out a little in his older years, but in the beginning he was cruel in ways I can't tell you. Michael is the one who started his investigation business by accident. For a time, he was working at a high-end restaurant and overheard a woman talking about a necklace that had been stolen. Using his usual charm and his ability to bluff, he convinced her to hire him to find it for her and that was the start of everything. He studied the antiques business and became affiliated with key contacts. He partnered with his cousin because that's the kind of man he is, but he was the one who made it a success, not that he'll ever admit that.

"His cousin was a failed businessman who piled up debt, got into trouble with some shady characters and made promises he rarely kept. But Michael doesn't see any of that because his cousin provided Michael a place to stay and that means everything to him." Darren stacked the dishes and drained the sink. "Do you know why he puts on the charm?"

Noreen shook her head.

Darren grabbed a dish towel and dried his hands. "Because he wants to be liked. That's his survival strategy. For years he lived in fear that his cousin would send him away as others had, but he made sure that Undy liked him and that others did too." Darren folded up the dishrag and placed it on the counter. "The reason why I'm telling you all this is because he cares about your sister and he wants to be part of your family. Your rejection will hurt him—he won't admit it, but it will. Just give him a chance. He may seem slick and shallow to you because he's quick to smile and crack a joke, but he's solid."

"He's also lucky to have a friend like you."

Darren shrugged then took a step toward her. "I make a good friend." He looked down. "I'm not sure this is the right time to ask, but would you like to have coffee sometime?"

Noreen wanted to refuse him, her feelings so raw that she didn't think she could go out ever again. But she liked him. She liked his quiet energy and serious, sweet gaze. Maybe in time she would forget Michael. "I'd love it."

"Great," he said and Noreen felt her flagging spirits lift a little.

Unfortunately, the man she wanted to forget burst into the room and looked at them with an unreadable look. "Sorry to interrupt," he said solemnly. "Darren, we need your help hanging a garland."

Darren hesitated, sending his friend an odd look. "The three of you can't hang a garland?"

Michael waited and a tense silence filled the room.

Noreen leaned toward Darren and said in a loud whisper. "You'd better go before he has a tantrum."

Darren smothered a grin then walked to the door that Michael held open. "Okay, I'll save the day."

"My hero," Noreen teased in simpering tones before she blew him a kiss.

Darren shook his head then left.

Michael shot Noreen a glance, but she couldn't read whether he was annoyed by her comment, her behavior or something else. She'd never seen that look on his face before. It was implacable. However, it didn't stop her from seeing him as a child desperately wanting to be liked so that he wouldn't be sent away. She imagined him charming clients so that he could make enough money to clear his cousin's bills. As she watched him she wanted to erase him from her heart, but all that Darren had said only made her love him more. Noreen steeled herself against her unwanted feelings and met his hard stare with one of her own.

"Did you need something else?" she asked him with more coldness than she'd meant to.

Michael blinked and something wary and vulnerable flickered in his eyes before it disappeared. "No, thanks," he said in a light tone that seemed false then he turned and left.

# Chapter 18

"What's wrong with you?" Darren demanded when he met Michael in the hallway.

Michael looked blank. "What do you mean?"

"You and I both know that you don't need my help to hang up some stupid garlands."

Michael started to walk past him, but Darren grabbed his arm and shoved him against the wall. He held up his thumb and forefinger in front of Michael's face. "You are this close to getting everything you want. In the other room is a beautiful, sexy woman who loves you and this is the start of a new life for you. Don't mess it up. I just finished trying to make things better between you and Noreen."

"Thank you."

"Don't thank me. Tell me what's going on. What

happened to the Vaughn charm? Okay, so her sister isn't as funny and bubbly as Arlene, but that doesn't mean you need to be a jerk."

Michael hung his head in disgust. "I know. I'm sorry. It's just…" He let his words trail off.

"It's what?" Darren pressed.

"Nothing. Forget it. Let's go." He pushed himself from the wall and walked away, effectively ending a conversation he didn't want to have. His friend was right. Something was wrong. With him. He'd discovered something about himself he'd never wanted to admit: he was a bastard. He thought he'd changed. He thought he was ready to settle down and not need the high and thrill of the chase. He'd been convinced even when his cousin wasn't.

"You? Settle down?" his cousin Undy had said as he lay in his hospital bed, recovering from surgery for removal of kidney stones. "No way."

"It's true," Michael said, leaning forward in his chair. "I'm a taken man."

"Taken for a ride maybe. But every ride has to end."

"Not this one."

"You're going to run out of gas and want to switch make and model. You've never been able to stay in one place long, especially when it comes to women. If you get too comfortable, you'll bolt. Remember, you tried with Joy and got antsy after only a few months."

"I'm different now and Joy wasn't the one."

Undy sniffed. "If a woman like that can't keep you satisfied—"

"Arlene is the woman for me. We understand each other. You'll know it when you meet her."

Undy was quiet a moment then said, "I want to believe you, but as I look at you, I know you can't change. You've never stayed constant with anything. You tried college and left. You tried staying with Joy and didn't. You even tried to retire from your work and couldn't. You're meant to be a free agent. Marriage isn't for everyone, and for you it will feel like a noose around your neck."

Michael faced that fact now as he helped Arlene string lights around the mantel. For months he'd thought about Arlene and proving his cousin wrong. He'd bought the island property they had talked about one day while lying on the beach, imagining how she would look when she saw it. He'd kept tabs on her and learned that she'd moved in with her sister.

He hadn't planned to "disappear" but after the way things ended on St. Lagans he wanted to take time and plan on how he would enter back into her life. The moment he'd stepped into Noreen's house he'd felt right about coming to her first and then he'd seen Arlene. After so many months she was still beautiful and her fun, sexy self. But what let him know his timing was perfect was the fact that she was still wearing the necklace he had given her.

Yet something was off and he didn't know what. Her sister Noreen's guarded glances bothered him. Her cool replies and refusal to spend any time with them in decorating the house grated his nerves. Her opinion mattered to him, no matter how much he didn't want it to. But what he found most disturbing was how Arlene's sister had become an alluring challenge. That was wrong. He was supposed to be over those feelings. What was wrong with him? Yes, they were identical twins, but the way they dressed and acted made them complete opposites.

But for some reason Noreen didn't just entice him as a challenge; she intrigued him and he hated that. Arlene was all that mattered and yet at times when she smiled at him it was as if he was a gallant knight who was the answer to all her dreams. Or like a child who was confident that she'd never be hurt again. Michael hadn't noticed that look before and he found himself uncomfortable in the role she'd given him and he wanted to run.

When Darren disappeared to join Noreen in the kitchen, all he could think about was what his friend was doing and if he'd had better luck thawing the ice queen than he'd had. When he couldn't contain his curiosity any longer, he'd gone into the kitchen and saw them together. Instead of being happy for his friend, he'd been struck with an irrational jealousy. Why had Noreen chosen Darren to offer her soft smiles and tenderness? Why did she make Darren feel like a guest and make him feel like an intruder? And why did he care? How come Noreen was suddenly making him see his best friend as a rival? *What was wrong with him?*

His ego was the problem, Michael tried to convince himself. He was so used to making people like him, that failure wasn't an option. Considering Arlene's history with men, he couldn't blame Noreen for not trusting him. And the way he'd met Arlene hadn't been under the best of circumstances. He had to accept that it would take time to win Noreen's acceptance, but he didn't plan on making Arlene's sister liking him or not a reason for not going forward.

Michael took a deep breath and looked over at Arlene as she held up two ornaments to her ears and pretended they were earrings, making Vince and Darren laugh. Ever since they'd met on the cruise he'd dreamed about nothing else but their future together, and he was going to make sure that came true.

"You've outdone yourself, Noreen," Vince said as they all sat down to dinner.

She'd made too much food, but cooking had kept her busy so she didn't mind. The table was filled with roasted chicken, mashed potatoes (both white and sweet), dinner rolls, salad, fish cakes, broccoli and cauliflower, sliced ham and cranberry sauce.

"I may never leave," Darren said, taking a seat across from her.

Michael didn't say anything as he sat at the table and Noreen did her best to ignore him, but that was impossible when she was forced to sit next to him. She had a small circular table because she rarely entertained and her thigh brushed against his.

"Sorry the table isn't bigger."

"Don't worry," Michael said. "Arlene and I are used to being crowded together." He reached for the fish cakes at the same time Noreen did, his hand covering hers. He yanked his hand away and looked at Arlene. "Remember that lunch on St. Barnaby?"

"Oh yes," she said. "That was fun. Show everyone the picture of the property you bought."

Noreen placed two fish cakes on his plate.

He stared at the food in front of him. "Maybe another time."

Arlene nudged him. "Please."

He reluctantly pulled out the picture and handed it to her.

She wiggled in her seat like a happy child. "It's so beautiful." She held the photo out to Vince. "Look, Dad."

He studied the photo, impressed. "How much?" Noreen kicked him under the table. "I mean, good choice."

"I've never seen Michael so determined to get something," Darren said. "You should have seen his face when he closed the deal." He smiled at Arlene. "Now I know why he was so eager."

Arlene blushed and Noreen blinked, surprised that Darren's comment affected her sister like that. "Dad, show Noreen."

Vince handed Noreen the photo and she barely glanced at it before handing it back to Michael. "Very nice."

Michael shoved the picture back inside his pocket. "How do you know?" he asked in a low voice. "You didn't look at it."

"Yes, I did."

"Forget it." He took a bite of the fish cake. "This tastes good."

"Thank you. I'm sure Arlene's taste better."

His jaw twitched but he didn't respond and Noreen regretted her comment. She was being petty and unfair. "Just wait until you try her sugar cookies. You'll feel like you've died and gone to heaven." After she said the word *heaven,* heat stole into her cheeks when she remembered their first night together.

Michael appeared to remember too, because he became still. "Good," he said, keeping his gaze focused on his food.

Noreen decided to focus on eating as well and she tried to be nonchalant when his leg or arm brushed against hers, but an electric thrill shot through her each time. She knew he couldn't help it because he was a big guy and the table was small. She promised herself that she would buy a long dining table tomorrow. Fortunately, no one noticed her discomfort.

Her sister sparkled and Noreen caught Darren watching her, which was no surprise, but what did surprise her was when she caught her father staring at her. At the end of the meal, Noreen stood and began to clear the table. Michael stood too. "Let me help you."

"No, I'm fine."

"It's no problem."

Noreen yanked the plate from him. "I said, I'm fine."

Michael sent her an odd look and sat down.

She looked at Darren and softened her tone. "But

thanks anyway. I want you all to just enjoy yourselves. I'm here to serve."

Noreen hurried into the kitchen, piling the dirty dishes on the counter.

"What a load of crock," her father said, entering the room.

"Crock?"

"Yes, all that you just said out there." He gestured to the dining room with his thumb. "I don't know what you have against the boy, but he's just trying to be friendly."

"I know, but he doesn't need to impress me. Arlene likes him—excuse me—loves him and apparently so do you."

"Yes, I do. I'm a player so I can easily spot them. He's not one. He's for real and I think he'll treat your sister well. He's certainly better than the other scum and deadbeats she used to bring home."

"I know."

"Of course, that's not good news for you."

Noreen looked at him, curious. "Why not?"

Vince walked over to the counter and rested against it. "Because *you're* in love with him."

Noreen turned away, unable to face her father, her heart racing.

"You can't fool me, Noreen. I see the way you look at him. What's going on?"

"Nothing."

"Does he know how you feel? Did she steal him away from you or something?"

"No. It doesn't matter. Arlene has him. Besides, there wouldn't even be a competition."

"You're just as beautiful and wonderful in your own way."

"Don't start with me, Dad. To you, all women are the same and you get bored, but you're not an exception. Most men are happy with whatever woman they get… at least for a while."

"Stop being a hypocrite."

Noreen stared at him. "What?"

"You heard me. You're not afraid that men think all women are the same—you're truly terrified that they don't. Otherwise you'd go into that room and take Michael for yourself."

"I—I," Noreen sputtered, unable to find any words.

He held up his hand. "Be quiet for a moment and listen. You think all men want women like your sister, but you're wrong. Just like women, all men aren't the same. For most of my life I've been an arrogant bastard. Women came easily. They still do. I never married because I got all that I wanted without the complications and legalities. But it's funny—when you get older, family starts to mean more. Besides, I hate seeing you hurt. You're my daughter, Noreen, and you're somebody special."

"Dad," Noreen said, not wanting to have this conversation now.

"I know we don't see eye to eye, but I love you. Your ex was no good. I'm glad he's gone. I'm happy Arlene's going to make me a grandfather. But I'd be just as glad to read your latest book."

"You never read my books."

"Yes, I do."

"They're romance," Noreen said, baffled. "You don't read romance."

"I've read yours. You can blame your grandmother for that. When she was in the nursing home I would go and read to her and she only wanted your books. I read one and got hooked, and after she died I continued reading them because they made me feel good. Your stories are about men with honor and integrity. Traits I didn't possess. They were, and still are, fun escapes. They taught me about love.

"I have had lots of fun but it was selfish love. Just like my father. And I raised three sons with the same values, men who go through women like water and are never satisfied. As you and your sister grew up, I came to see you for the women you are. I think somehow I'm being punished, because I hate to see my daughters treated the way I've treated other men's daughters. I have two daughters I cherish and hurt. One who tries to find love anywhere she can and another who's given up on it completely. Even when it's staring her in the face."

Noreen held back tears. "He belongs to Arlene."

"Maybe, but Arlene doesn't look at him the way you do when you think no one is watching." Vince was silent a moment then said, "You switched places, didn't you?" When she didn't respond immediately, he grinned. "Yes, you did, and for the first time it backfired. Go. Tell him how you feel."

"There's no point."

Vince stood in front of her. "I know I haven't been a good father—"

"It's okay, Dad. I'm okay, really. I don't want him. I don't need him. I don't need anyone. I've got my friends and my career is back on schedule. I want to see my sister happy so I can get on with my life. Now please go back to my guests while I figure out dessert."

Vince kissed his daughter on the forehead then whispered, "You lie as well as I do," then left.

Once he was gone, Noreen gripped the counter and shut her eyes. Was she that obvious? Too much was at stake. Arlene's happiness. Michael's trust. It would be better when they left. Hopefully that would be soon and they would decide to elope.

Noreen filled a pot with water to begin preparing dessert. As she lifted the pot out of the sink she heard someone enter. "Do you have more advice, Dad?"

"No," Michael said.

Noreen kept her back to him and gripped the pot tighter. "Oh. Did you need something?"

"I want to talk to you."

"So talk," she said in a thin voice, feeling emotionally exhausted.

"I know you don't like me."

Noreen spun around. "That's not true."

"Yes, it is."

"No, it's not."

Michael held out his hands. "Let's not argue about it. I understand why you wouldn't trust me, whether you want to admit it or not, but I don't care what you think about me right now. But I do care about Arlene and how she feels and you're hurting her and I won't allow that."

Noreen's mouth fell open. "You won't *allow* that? How dare you come into my home and tell me how to behave? Where were you two months ago when my sister came back with a broken heart? Where were the notes or letters or emails letting her know where you were or how you felt? What about a phone call or at least a message?" Noreen's voice trembled as tears gathered in her eyes. "Where were you when she woke up from a nightmare or called your name out in a dream? You weren't here to pick up the pieces, but I was."

Michael took a step toward her then stopped, curling his hands into fists. "I'm sorry." He rubbed his forehead. "I know Arlene's been hurt, lied to and used in the past, and I wasn't a good example of how she should be treated. But if you know how I feel about her, you would know what happened is all in the past. I will cherish her, care for her and love her until my dying day."

Noreen glanced away, feeling her arms begin to ache. "I'm sure you will."

"You don't believe me."

She looked at him. "What does it matter what I believe? Darren's happy for you. You've impressed my father and my sister is madly in love with you. What more do you want? Tell her your beautiful sentiments. Make all your promises to her and leave me alone." Noreen altered her grip, nearly dropping the pot.

Michael rushed over to her and grabbed the handle. "Let me help you."

Noreen tightened her hold. "I'm fine."

"It weighs nearly as much as you do."

"Let go."

"No."

"I told you to leave me alone."

"Fine," Michael said, releasing his hold.

He let go just as Noreen was pulling the pot toward her and the water splashed, soaking her face and shirt. He swore and looked at her with a guilty expression. "I'm really sorry about that."

Noreen looked at him, all her frustration reaching the boiling point. She threw the remaining water on him. "I'm really sorry too."

Michael looked down at the puddle of water at his feet then met her eyes. They looked at each other for a long moment then burst into laughter.

Arlene, Darren and Vince appeared in the doorway. "What's going on in here?" Vince asked.

Michael bit his lip while Noreen covered her mouth, trying to stifle her laughter, but then they shared a look and started laughing again.

"Have you two gone crazy?" Vince asked as Darren and Arlene looked at them, baffled.

Michael pointed at Noreen. "It's all her fault."

Noreen took off her glasses and wiped them. "My fault? You splashed me first."

"That was an accident." Michael quickly unbuttoned and removed his shirt and wrung it out over the sink. "Yours was deliberate."

"Guilty," Noreen admitted, unable to stop her gaze from scanning his bare chest. She noticed a violent scar left by the accident on his back. "Have you been applying the vitamin E on that? I'm surprised it's still so prominent," she said, touching it lightly with her fingers. "I thought after two months it would be gone by now."

Michael froze and a sudden tense silence filled the room. At that moment Noreen knew the weight of her mistake.

He turned to her, his hazel eyes intense and probing. "What did you just say?"

Noreen looked over at her sister, whose sweet brown gaze pleaded for her to lie; then she looked up at Michael, whose unrelenting gaze demanded the truth. Noreen stared up at him, unable to speak.

A sob escaped Arlene and she ran out of the room. Darren followed her.

Noreen broke out of her paralysis and called out to her sister. "Wait!"

Michael blocked her. "What's going on?"

Noreen looked at her father, feeling helpless.

"Tell him," he said.

Michael searched her face. "Tell me what?"

Noreen sighed, knowing her moment of reckoning had come.

## Chapter 19

"I have something I need to explain."

Michael dropped his soggy shirt into the sink and rested his hand on the counter. "Is this explanation going to help me understand why I've felt like a fraud all evening? Why I've felt like a complete bastard because even though I've thought about Arlene for months, and she looks at me with adoring eyes like I'm some rescuing knight here to take care of her, it's not enough?"

He took a step closer. "Are you going to explain why the entire time I've been with Arlene this evening I haven't been able to stop thinking of you? What you were doing? What you thought of me? What you would taste like if I kissed you?" His eyes dropped to her lips. "I still wonder." He lifted his gaze and met her eyes. "Can you explain all that?"

Noreen swallowed, staring into his sharp, intelligent eyes. "I think you already know."

"I want to hear you say it."

"I'm Arlene. I mean, I was."

Michael folded his arms, his eyes dark. "I'm listening."

"My sister and I switched places. I agreed to go on the cruise and deliver the antique so that she could go see a doctor and find out if she was pregnant. I thought it was a good idea at first and then it got…um…complicated. When I saw you again, at first I wanted to tell you, but you had fallen for Arlene and cared about her, not me and I—"

Michael stopped her words with a kiss and Noreen stiffened, expecting it to be punishing and angry, but it wasn't. It was a savage vow, a declaration of possession she couldn't deny. Her heart, her soul, her body would belong to no other man but him, and she surrendered to that revelation. She wrapped her arms around him, letting her hands explore the sleek, bare flesh beneath her fingers.

He moaned with pleasure. "Oh yes, that feels right. I've wanted to hold you for so long." His mouth slid to her neck. "You little witch," he said in a low, husky voice.

Noreen grinned. "I thought I was an angel."

"I think you're both." He tenderly kissed her. "I missed you so much. I wish I could have come to you sooner but aside from my cousin getting sick, Alvarez escaped."

Noreen stiffened with fear. "He did?"

Michael stroked her cheek as his tender gaze roamed over her face. "Don't worry, Angel. He'll never hurt you again. I made sure."

"How?"

His eyes briefly turned cold. "Do you really want to know?"

She shook her head. Whatever had happened to Alvarez had been deserved.

"Good," Michael said then kissed her again and slipped his hand under her wet shirt, cupping her breast.

Noreen leaned into him, pressing her lips on his chest then abruptly stopped as a thought came to her. "Wait, we can't do this."

"Why not?"

"Because Arlene and my father are in the other room, not to mention Darren."

"You're right. Where's your bedroom?"

"No, that's not what I mean." Noreen removed his exploring hands and pulled away from him, feeling miserable. "My sister is going to hate me." Noreen blinked back tears. "She needs you. You saw her. You care about her. I can take care of myself, but she's going to have a baby and I've messed up everything."

Michael rested his hands on her shoulders. "No, you haven't. I like Arlene a lot, but I want you."

Noreen shook her head. "Michael, what you want is an illusion. I'm nothing like the woman you met on the cruise. I work too hard and worry too much. I live in this house, which wouldn't have been decorated if it hadn't been for Arlene." Noreen looked down at her jeans and shirt. "This is how I dress. I'm a writer and I have an ex-husband who thinks I'm as exciting as porridge. I pay my taxes early and I go to bed late. And…what's so funny?" she asked, catching his smile.

"You're rambling."

"I know. I'm sorry."

His smile grew. "No, that's what I missed."

She frowned. "Missed?"

"Yes. When I was with Arlene she never once rambled on and that's because she wasn't you."

"Exactly. Arlene doesn't ramble and she doesn't worry. Even Darren's fallen for her. I don't blame him. She's easygoing, and fun and impulsive and—"

"She won't be single for long."

"I know," Noreen said with a groan. "She'll fall for the next man who pays any attention to her."

"I hope so. She'll make Darren very happy."

Noreen paused. "What about you?"

"What about me?"

"Don't you want her too?"

"I want the woman who was there when I was hit by a car. The one who took the stage on karaoke night." A wicked smiled touched his lips. "And sang with me in the shower. That's the only woman I want to be with. Is that you?"

Noreen blushed and nodded.

Michael's gaze grew serious as his finger trailed a sensuous path down her jaw. "You better get your necklace back. I don't ever want to see your sister wearing it again. Agreed?"

"Agreed," Noreen said, sensing the pain her betrayal

had caused him. His mother's necklace was something he treasured. "I'm sorry."

"I'll only believe you if you'll marry me."

"That's blackmail."

"No, it's a question."

She opened her mouth wanting to say yes, but then fear entered. She wanted him to promise that he'd never leave her, that he'd never become tired of her. She remembered her ex making the same promises and then walking out of her life just as her mother had.

Noreen bit her lip. "You're wonderful."

"That's not an answer."

She was afraid to trust when everything between them had been a lie. She continued to look at him but her throat closed.

Michael let his arms fall and lowered his eyes in defeat. "All right. I understand." He turned and walked out the door.

Noreen let him go and turned to clean up the mess of water before leaving the kitchen. She went into the family room where Vince, Arlene and Darren sat.

She looked at her sister, feeling guilty. "Are you all right?"

"I'm fine," she said, all signs of distress gone. "It wouldn't have worked anyway."

Noreen felt relieved that her sister was okay and, seeing how close she sat next to Darren, Noreen knew he was part of the reason why. She tugged on her soggy shirt. "I'm just going to go change." She looked around, confused. "Where's Michael?"

"He left," Arlene said.

"What?"

Darren shook his head. "He—"

Arlene interrupted him. "Grabbed his coat and left without saying goodbye. He's getting in his car now."

Noreen looked out the window and watched him, knowing that in seconds he would drive out of her life forever. She was terrified of being abandoned, of being betrayed, but everything about their time together hadn't been a lie. Their feelings for each other were real. She looked around the room at the glowing lights, the candy canes and stars. It was a season of miracles. She may not believe in Santa Claus or reindeers that fly or ghosts but she did believe in love.

Noreen ran outside, not caring how the cold threatened to turn her wet shirt into ice or how the wind stung her cheeks. "*Te quiero mucho,* Miguel," she blurted.

Michael spun around.

She wrung her hands, feeling bare and vulnerable but not caring. "Please don't leave. I'll marry you."

Michael's extraordinary eyes blazed and glowed with a love that was almost blinding, and at that moment Noreen knew he'd been just as afraid and unsure. All her fears melted away.

"I wasn't leaving," he said. "I was getting a shirt from inside my car." He disappeared inside and pulled one out and showed her. "I keep an extra in a carrying case."

Noreen started to shiver from both embarrassment and cold. "Oh."

He unzipped his coat and drew her inside his arms,

transferring his heat to her. "Did you mean what you first said?"

"Every word," she said, feeling the ice on her shirt melt away. *"Te quiero mucho."*

He said a series of passionate words, which she couldn't understand before he kissed her in a way that was raw and real and needed no translation. He cupped her face. "My darling Angel," he whispered against her lips. "I'm never letting you go."

Noreen grinned. "My darling Pirate. I'm forever yours."

Claudia Madison nearly choked on her breakfast when she read Noreen's email. She read it twice to make sure she'd read it correctly then called her friend Suzanne Gordon.

"Is it April Fools' Day or something?" she asked.

"No," Suzanne replied with a laugh.

"But this has to be a trick. This doesn't sound like sensible Noreen at all."

"No, but she's happy and that's all that matters," Suzanne said then reread the email with a smile.

Dear Claudia and Suzanne,
You're not going to believe this, but I've gone and married myself a pirate. He bought me a lovely house on a Caribbean island (I've attached pictures), where we plan to live six months out of the year. I never thought I'd be able to love again, but you were right, my dear friends, heartbreak isn't fatal and true love is the best cure. You'll get to

meet Michael soon. For now, don't worry about me, I'm having the time of my life.
All the best,
Noreen Vargas

\* \* \* \* \*

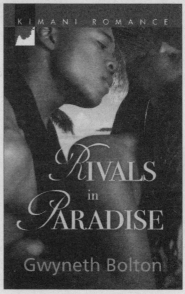

# REQUEST YOUR FREE BOOKS!

## 2 FREE NOVELS
## PLUS 2 FREE GIFTS!

KIMANI™
ROMANCE

### Love's ultimate destination!

KROM10R

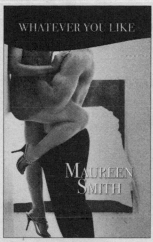

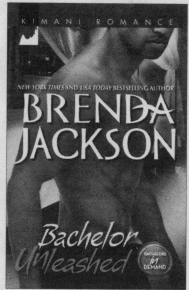